PRAISE FOR JEFF STRAND'S *IT WATCHES IN THE DARK*

"Sure to spike curiosity in young readers."

—*Youth Services Book Review*

"[A] darkly comic, Goosebumps-esque tale."

—*Publishers Weekly*

"The resourcefulness, cooperation, and affection displayed by the twins offset some truly scary moments, and a genuinely surprising ending provides macabre humor."

—*Kirkus Reviews*

JEFF STRAND
NIGHTMARE IN THE BACKYARD
EEK!
sourcebooks
young readers

Copyright © 2024 by Jeff Strand
Cover and internal design © 2024 by Sourcebooks
EEK! branding © 2024 by Sourcebooks
Cover design by Michelle Mayhall / Sourcebooks
Cover and internal art © 2024 by David Seidman
Internal design by Jessica Nordskog / Sourcebooks

Published by Sourcebooks Young Readers, an imprint of Sourcebooks
P.O. Box 4410, Naperville, Illinois 60567-4410
(630) 961-3900
sourcebooks.com

Cataloging-in-Publication Data is on file with the Library of Congress.

This product conforms to all applicable CPSC and CPSIA standards.

Source of Production: Maple Press, York, Pennsylvania, USA
Date of Production: May 2024
Tradepaper ISBN: 9781728277660. Run Number: 5038285
Hardcover ISBN: 9781728277639. Run Number 5038284

Printed and bound in the United States of America.
MA 10 9 8 7 6 5 4 3 2 1

To Bridgett. Let's fight monsters together!

CHAPTER 1

"I'm going to murder this tent," said Chloe Whitting.

"I'll help you," said her best friend, Avery Gonzalez, crawling out of the entrance.

The tent package promised, EASY SETUP. The tent was not, in fact, easy to set up. The instructions were impossible to decipher, like ancient cave art drawn by someone who'd gotten distracted by a hungry bear. Arrows pointed to parts that didn't seem to exist. What was step seven even asking them to do?

Though Chloe wanted to find a pair of scissors and cut the tent into a thousand very tiny pieces of blue vinyl, she resisted the urge to destroy it. They were going to have an amazing night camping out in her backyard. She and Avery were going to roast marshmallows over the firepit, tell ghost stories, play games, and talk all night in their sleeping bags, if they ever got the tent up. Otherwise, they might just sleep on the ground, using anthills as pillows.

Dad probably could've put up this tent in three minutes, but... Chloe didn't want to think about that right now. It was part of the reason she really needed tonight. This past year had been hard without him around. She needed some fun, and summer was just about over.

Tonight would be fun. It would be like a real camping trip, but unlike the family camping trips they took every year, they could go inside when they needed to use the bathroom. They wouldn't have to bathe in a cold river. And there'd be no wild animals, apart from the occasional squirrel. Yeah, they'd hear cars driving by, and there wouldn't be any hiking to get to their campsite, and Dad's "no cell phones" rule wouldn't be in effect, but aside from that, it would be exactly like a real wilderness camping trip.

Most of her neighbors were hidden anyway. The neighbor behind their house had a great big wooden fence, as did the neighbor to one side. (Both of those families had dogs. Since Chloe's mom was allergic to both dogs and cats, her only pet was an iguana named Ziggy.) Her other next-door neighbors were the Duncans. You could tell where the property line was because the Duncans didn't mow their lawn as often.

The back door swung open, and Mom came outside. "How's the tent-building going?"

"We're done," said Avery, gesturing to the pile of tent pieces. "What do you think, Mrs. Whitting? *Perfecto*, right?"

"It's these instructions," Chloe said. She walked over to Mom and handed the instructions to her. "Here, look. It's like you need an engineering degree."

Mom's eyebrows furrowed. "What does step seven even mean?"

"I don't know! It would be easier to fix the tree house!"

The tree house was supposed to be a present for Chloe's seventh birthday, but Dad wasn't much of a carpenter, and she'd been eight before it was ready. She'd done a lot of reading and drawing there, and her scrapbook was probably still up there. The weather hadn't been kind to it, though, and four years later, she wouldn't go up there without positioning her trampoline to catch her in case she broke through the floorboards.

"Well, I'm sure that if the sisters work together, you can figure it out," said Mom.

Chloe and Avery weren't sisters. They definitely didn't *look* like sisters. Chloe, who was short for her age, had curly red hair and freckles galore. She wore thick lime-colored glasses that gave her a nerdy look she was proud of. Avery was the tallest girl in class and had straight black hair that went down to her waist. But they'd known each other since kindergarten and acted so much like siblings that Chloe's mom had taken to calling them "the sisters."

"I don't know what you mean," said Avery, lifting the collapsed part of the tent with her foot. "It's done, right?"

Mom laughed but didn't go back inside.

"What's wrong?" asked Chloe.

"Nothing's wrong." Her mother shifted her weight between her feet.

"Okay, but you're still here, looking like you have something to say."

"Nope."

"Still here..."

"Right," said Mom. "It's no big deal. I came out to check on how the tent was going and, uh, to let you know that Aunt Sandy is coming over tonight. For our own little sleepover."

"Mom! No!"

Chloe didn't mind Aunt Sandy visiting. Aunt Sandy was

her only aunt and would surely have been her favorite aunt if there'd been any competition. What Chloe did mind, very much, was that Aunt Sandy always brought along Chloe's cousin, Madison.

There were times when Madison was perfectly fine to have around. Shopping trips. Restaurant meals. Movie night at home, as long as she got the recliner. Madison was way less fun when it came to sports (physical activity was not really her thing), fishing ("Ew! Ew! Ew!"), and, of course, camping.

Chloe wanted to talk about boys *some* of the time. She did not want to talk about boys *all* the time. But aside from discussing clothing, Madison didn't seem to care about anything else.

"It'll be fun," Mom promised.

"Oh, so she's leaving Madison at home?"

Mom gave her a pointed look.. "She's your cousin, and your aunt is going through a rough time. You know that."

"Yes, I'm sorry Aunt Sandy broke up with her boyfriend. I can't think of anything worse than that, except maybe *Dad disappearing without a trace.* You know, when Dad didn't come home from work one night, and we never heard from him again? That was pretty rough, huh?"

Chloe closed her eyes, inhaled deeply, held her breath

for a few moments, and exhaled. She carried a lot of anger within her. She tried to let it go. She didn't want to fight with Mom. She wanted to enjoy the night, during the last weekend before school started again, and getting mad that Madison was crashing their camping trip would not help her achieve that goal.

She opened her eyes.

Avery, who'd helped her through a lot of the anger she'd felt this last year, stepped over and put a hand on her shoulder.

"It's fine," said Chloe. "I'm sorry."

She already knew the answer to *can't Madison stay inside with you?* Even if she hated what Chloe found fun and constantly reminded her of it, Madison always wanted to be included.

Mom forced a smile. "I'm sure she'll be on her best behavior. She's much more mature now."

"We're the same age. And I saw her last week."

"Still..."

"It's totally okay to have Madison here," Avery chimed in.

Chloe took the cue from her friend. There was no reason to turn this into an argument. She sighed. "It'll be nice to have her join us."

"Thank you." Mom seemed to relax. She gave Chloe's shoulder a squeeze and then walked back inside.

Chloe sighed again.

"Madison isn't so bad," said Avery.

"I know, I know. I just wanted this to be perfect."

"It'll still be perfect. Except for this tent! Can we burn it?"

/////

They eventually got the tent up, although it required three separate YouTube instructional videos. The top still sagged, but they weren't being graded, so it was fine.

Chloe and Avery crawled into the tent. With only the two of them, there would have been plenty of room. Adding Madison would make the space cramped, but they'd survive. They rolled out their sleeping bags and lay on top of them.

In the quiet, Chloe couldn't help but think of her dad. He would have loved this. That blanket of worry and fear that had been so familiar this past year settled over her body. She took a long, slow breath, but she couldn't shake it off. So much for distraction. She shifted on her sleeping bag.

"Ow, there's a lump," said Chloe.

"Really?" asked Avery. "We checked that the ground was level before we set up the tent."

Chloe sat up and patted her sleeping bag. "Yeah, there's something under there."

"Oh well. We'll just take down the tent and set it up again. No biggie."

Chloe laughed. "Yeah, right." She pushed her sleeping bag out of the way and slid her hand along the vinyl. "Wait, now I can't feel it."

"Good."

"That's weird. There was definitely something under my sleeping bag."

"Maybe it was a groundhog or a mole," said Avery. "Or you're the girl from 'The Princess and the Pea.'"

"Seriously, I didn't imagine it. I have no idea what it was, but it was there."

"Is it inside your sleeping bag?"

Chloe ran her hands over the sleeping bag, top to bottom. "Nope."

Avery checked the floor of the tent. "Well, there's nothing there now."

"I didn't make it up."

"I don't think you made anything up. But the phantom lump is gone."

"That's strange," said Chloe. "I guess it's no big deal. We have more important things to talk about. Do you have your scary story ready?"

Avery nodded. "Mine will make your hair turn white. You'll have three or four heart attacks. You'll scream for at least seventeen hours after you hear it."

Chloe smiled. She loved being around Avery. "Cool."

The back door creaked open, so Chloe and Avery crawled out of the tent. It was Mom, Aunt Sandy, and Madison. Madison was appropriately dressed for a backyard campout—if that campout were a beauty pageant instead. Her blond hair had been perfectly styled, and she was even wearing makeup. Chloe supposed they might play around with some makeup later, but no one was supposed to show up looking like a fashion model ready to walk the runway.

"Hi, Aunt Sandy," said Chloe. "Hi, Madison."

"Hi," said Aunt Sandy. "I like your tent. It's cute."

"Thanks," said Avery. "It was really easy to put up."

"Did you bring pajamas?" Chloe asked Madison.

Madison nodded. "Four pairs."

"Why four?"

"I didn't know what color the tent would be."

"I'll go get your cot," said Aunt Sandy, then headed back inside the house.

Chloe and Avery exchanged a glance.

"Did she say she was getting your cot?" Chloe asked.

"Yeah," said Madison. "Mom doesn't want me to hurt my back sleeping on the ground."

"That's very considerate of her," said Chloe, without enthusiasm.

The tent wasn't intended to accommodate a cot and two sleeping bags, but she supposed it could be worse. Madison could've brought her four-poster bed from home.

"Also, there are bugs on the ground," said Madison. "You know, spiders and beetles and centipedes and stuff. Have you ever been bitten by a centipede?"

"Nope," said Chloe.

"Have you ever been bitten by a centipede, Avery?"

"I can't say that I have."

"Neither have I. But it sounds terrible. Their bites can cause severe swelling, redness, and pain."

"Redness is the worst," said Chloe.

"Oh, I know," said Madison, not recognizing Chloe's sarcasm, as was typical of her. "People think centipedes aren't

10

dangerous because they look so cuddly with all those legs, but it's not true at all."

"*Do* centipedes look cuddly?" asked Chloe. "That's not the first word that comes to mind."

"What word comes to mind?" Avery asked.

"Squishable."

"You shouldn't squish a centipede," said Madison. "You could get their poison all over you. Besides, they're living creatures."

Chloe grimaced. "You'll be happy to know that our tent came equipped with an actual bottom, so the bugs won't be able to get in and bite us."

"They could get in through the main entrance when we're going in and out."

"Okay, yes, that's true," said Avery. "We're in serious danger from the centipede menace. We'll be careful."

Aunt Sandy emerged from the house, carrying a very large cot. It was pink, which was not a surprise.

Because the sides of the tent sagged, Aunt Sandy put the cot right in the center, forcing Chloe and Avery to scoot their sleeping bags to either side of it. This wasn't ideal, but the pizza had been delivered, so Chloe decided not to dwell on it, and they all went inside.

By the time the girls had devoured the pizza (double pepperoni, extra cheese), it was almost dark. With Mom and Aunt Sandy's close supervision, Chloe built a fire in the firepit. The adults were banished to the house, and the three girls sat around the fire, roasting marshmallows.

"Smoke is getting in my eyes," said Madison.

"Move your chair," Chloe told her.

Madison moved her chair. The breeze shifted. "It's following me."

Chloe's marshmallow caught fire and turned into a blackened mess, just the way she liked it. She pulled off the top crunchy layer, popped it into her mouth, and thrust the remainder back into the fire.

Avery held up her perfectly toasted marshmallow. "Are you ready for a tale...of *terror*?"

"We should wait for it to get a little darker," said Chloe.

Avery shook her head. "This tale is too scary for total darkness. You don't want to trip when you run away screaming. Also, y'know..."

She pointed to the house. The light above the back door was on, illuminating the backyard. Chloe's mom had insisted on this. It kind of spoiled the mood, but Chloe's protests hadn't worked.

"I'm ready," said Madison, whose marshmallow had been held a safe distance from the flames and looked barely warmed.

"Then prepare yourself," said Avery, "for the tale of The Man with No Head..."

CHAPTER 2

"Is this like 'The Legend of Sleepy Hollow'?" asked Chloe.

"No," said Avery. "It's a headless man, but not a headless *horse*man."

"Carry on," said Chloe.

Avery turned on her cell phone flashlight and held it under her chin.

"What are you doing?" asked Chloe.

"Spooky lighting."

"You can't really tell because of the fire."

Avery smiled. "Are you going to be like this for the whole story?"

"You know I am."

"Do you want a marshmallow in the face?"

"Will it be on fire?"

"Maybe."

"Then no. I'll behave," Chloe promised. She ran her fingers over her mouth like she was zipping her lips.

Madison raised an eyebrow, shook her head, and then delicately removed the marshmallow from her skewer and ate it.

Avery turned off the flashlight and tucked her cell phone back into her pocket. "His name was Jasper Gale," she began with a dramatic flair. "He was born with two arms, two legs, and one head, but the luxury of having a head wouldn't last forever. During a trip to a museum, he was walking through a medieval exhibit when he stumbled into some velvet ropes.

"Unfortunately for Jasper, he knocked into a suit of armor and—*slice*! Its sword came down and severed his head from his neck. His head rolled around for a while before coming to a stop."

"Ew," said Madison.

"Jasper was not an observant man," said Avery. "He was so unobservant that his body didn't notice his head had gotten chopped off. So he kept walking, even though he was slipping and sliding on his own blood. The guards and other visitors were terrified and fled. But Jasper kept walking. He bumped into a woolly mammoth—"

Chloe interrupted. "A real woolly mammoth?"

"No, a regular mammoth with a wig."

"Got it."

"Eventually Jasper found his way out of the museum and down the street. And people were so scared to see a headless man that they got distracted, and then *they* started accidentally walking into sharp things, and suddenly there were dismembered heads all over the place!

"Heads, heads, everywhere! You could barely take a step without kicking somebody's head like it was a soccer ball."

"Could the heads talk?" asked Madison.

"It's rude to interrupt somebody when they're telling a story," Chloe noted.

"Yes, the heads could talk," said Avery. "So, yeah, you'd be walking down the street, and there would be all these talking heads saying, 'Ow! My neck!' and 'Can you please lower your voice? I have a headache.' The city had to hire extra sanitation workers to sweep them up and bus drivers to take the heads and bodies to their homes. And then, one day—"

"*Bewaaaaaaaare!*" a ghostly voice moaned.

Madison screamed.

Avery screamed.

Chloe screamed and flung her marshmallow skewer in the direction of the voice.

"Whoa!" somebody cried out. "You almost hit me with that!"

"Elijah!" Chloe shouted.

Her neighbor Elijah Duncan stepped into the circle. He was a year older than the girls, and it was completely like him to sneak over and try to scare them like this. Chloe'd had a crush on him when she was ten and he was eleven, but she was long over it.

"You ruined my story," Avery told him. "I was just getting to the good part."

"Sorry, but I couldn't resist," said Elijah. "It was funny, right?"

"It would've been funnier if the skewer had gotten you in the eye," said Chloe.

"Look, if you're going to tell scary stories around the campfire, you have to expect somebody will jump out at you," said Elijah. "That's the way it works."

"He has a point," said Madison. "Pull up a chair and join us."

"There aren't any more chairs," said Elijah.

"Go get one."

"No," said Chloe. "Don't go get a chair. There are only three here for a reason."

"Madison invited me to join you."

"Avery and I outvoted her. And it's my house."

"I didn't hear Avery tell me to go home."

"Go home," said Avery.

Elijah picked up the skewer Chloe had thrown and handed it back to her. "All right, fine," he said reluctantly. He walked back into his yard, stopped right at the edge of his property line, and turned in the shadows, beyond the reach of the light.

"Are you being serious right now?" Chloe asked.

"I'm in my own yard."

"We're trying to have a campout."

"I'm not stopping you."

"Do you want me to tell your mom and dad you're being creepy?"

"I'm not being creepy," Elijah insisted. "I'm standing in my yard...in the dark...watching you..."

Chloe flung a marshmallow at him. It was a good throw, but the marshmallow had poor aerodynamic qualities and landed at his feet. Elijah picked it up and popped it into his mouth.

"Gross," said Avery.

"What?" Elijah asked. "Five-second rule. Ants are good protein."

"Seriously," said Chloe. "You scared us, and it was funny, and now it's time for you to go back inside and live your life."

"All right, I'll go. But at two in the morning, when you hear somebody scratching the side of your tent, you'd better hope it's me and not a serial killer!" He walked toward his house.

"Bye, Elijah!" Madison called out.

"Bye, Maddy!" Elijah called back. Light spilled out of his back door as he went inside.

"He calls you 'Maddy'?" asked Chloe.

"I guess he does. I like it."

"You're welcome to go hang out with him tonight if you want."

"Yeah, right. My mom would kill me." But Madison twisted a lock of hair around her finger like she was thinking about it.

"If he comes back, we need to scare him way worse than he did us," said Chloe. "Did anyone bring a Halloween mask?"

"No," said Avery.

"Chain saw?"

"No."

"I guess there isn't time to dig a swimming pool moat between the yards and put a shark in it."

"Probably not."

"He wasn't hurting anybody," said Madison. "I bet he has some good scary stories."

"Yeah, stories about his *face!*" said Chloe. Although, to be fair, Elijah had a perfectly nice face and perfectly nice spiky black hair. Too bad he was so annoying. Also lazy—his parents had to constantly remind him that it was time to mow the lawn. She turned to Avery. "Finish your story. What happens next?"

"I don't know," Avery admitted. "I was making it up as I went along. The heads probably went on a rampage or something."

"Your turn, Madison," said Chloe.

Madison nodded and leaned closer to the flames. "This happened many years ago. A lonely truck driver picked up a hitchhiker and brought him into town. The driver was going to get some food, and the hitchhiker recommended the local diner, but he asked to get dropped off before that. When he got out of the truck, the hitchhiker said, 'Tell them Donnie sent you.' So, the driver went to the diner, and he told them about Donnie, and everybody got quiet and scared because Donnie had died twenty years ago."

Chloe and Avery stared at her.

"He was a ghost," Madison explained.

The girls continued to stare.

"He was a *ghost*! He was in his truck with a ghost that whole time. Come on. Nothing? How would you feel if you gave somebody a ride and found out that they were dead? You'd be all like 'Ahhh! Ahhhh! It was a ghost!' Don't pretend you wouldn't be scared."

"Oh, I'd totally freak out," Chloe admitted. "You kinda stampeded right to the twist ending, though."

Madison shrugged. "I got nervous."

"I remember what I was going to say now!" said Avery. "The heads all joined together into one gigantic creature—a cranium creature—and it walked around eating people."

"What about the heads that were on the bottom?" asked Chloe. "The skulls that were its feet. What did they think about what was happening?"

"They hated it. Their faces kept getting smooshed into the ground and there was nothing they could do about it. Eventually, the cranium creature walked into the ocean, where it lives to this very day. So if you're ever on a cruise ship and you look out at the water, and you see the top of somebody's head, and you think that somebody fell overboard, beware, because it just may be the cranium creature, returning for vengeance."

"Yikes," said Madison.

Chloe scrunched up her face. "What does it have to avenge? It sounds like it went into the ocean on its own terms."

Avery rolled her eyes. "Let's hear your story then."

"No way," said Chloe. "I've spent all this time making fun of your stories. I'm not going to subject myself to that."

The girls all laughed. Then they toasted more marshmallows.

/////

"That was too many marshmallows," moaned Avery. "I feel like I'm going to throw up."

"They seemed so fluffy and harmless while we were eating them," said Chloe. "I guess we shouldn't have eaten the entire bag."

"We ate the entire bag?" asked Madison.

"Except the one I threw at Elijah, yeah."

"That wasn't very smart of us."

"No, it wasn't." Chloe stood up. Then she felt even queasier. "I'm going to get some water to douse the fire."

She went inside, staggering a bit. Their back door led

directly into the kitchen, so she took a pitcher out of the cupboard and turned on the faucet. "It's just me," she called out.

"Are you having fun?" Mom called back from the family room.

"We're out of control. We ate the entire bag of marshmallows."

"Why would you do that?" asked Aunt Sandy.

"I don't know. We've basically gone feral."

"Well, make sure you put out the fire before you go to bed," replied Mom.

"That's why I'm running the water."

Chloe filled up the pitcher, went back outside, and poured it on the fire. It made a satisfying *hiss* as she extinguished the flames.

The girls unzipped the tent and crawled inside.

"Don't puke in the tent," Chloe warned the others. "That goes for me too. And now...pajama time!"

Everybody changed into their pajamas.

"My clothes smell like smoke," said Madison.

They tossed their clothes out of the tent to air out, then zipped up the door. Madison got on her cot, while Chloe and Avery each lay on their own sleeping bags.

Suddenly it was very quiet with only the sounds of

crickets and their breathing. The floodlight created an eerie glow within the tent.

"What now?" Avery whispered with a shiver that didn't seem related to the weather.

"Let's talk about Elijah," said Madison.

"That's a great idea," said Chloe. "Another option is that we could talk about literally anybody or anything else."

"Ugh," said Avery, sitting up with a jolt.

"I agree," said Chloe. "Elijah is totally *ugh*."

"No, something moved under my sleeping bag. A moving lump."

"Really?"

Avery scooted her sleeping bag to the side and patted along the bottom of the tent. "It's gone again."

"What do you mean, 'gone *again*'?" Madison asked, worry creeping into her voice.

"When we were setting up the tent, I felt a lump under my sleeping bag," said Chloe. "And when Avery checked, there was no sign of it. But I know I didn't imagine it."

"Maybe it's a head," said Madison.

"Ha ha."

"Do you want to trade spots?" asked Chloe.

"Yes," said Avery. "Because if the traveling lump comes

back, I want you to feel it so you know I'm not making it up."

Chloe and Avery moved their sleeping bags.

"Do you think Elijah will try to scare us again?" Madison asked.

"It's not a choice that I would make if I were him," said Chloe. "The first time, I threw a marshmallow at him. The next time, I'll throw a brick."

"The first time, you threw a skewer," Madison pointed out.

"Okay, true. The first time, I threw a skewer; the second time, I threw a marshmallow; and the third time, I'll throw a brick. Or my shoe. Whatever's within reach. Either way, he'd better stay in his yard."

"Why don't you like him?"

"Because he—" Chloe frowned as something brushed against her foot. Then something slid beneath her.

Chloe gasped and scooted away. Her heart pounded in her chest. Something was underneath the tent. It kind of looked like a snake.

Then the shape disappeared, as if whatever it was went back into the ground.

CHAPTER 3

"Did you see that?" Chloe asked.

Avery frantically nodded. "What was that? A snake?"

"It was too big to be a snake!"

"It could've been a boa constrictor!"

"There are no boa constrictors around here!" Actually, Chloe didn't really know where boa constrictors lived, but she was pretty sure they weren't slithering around suburban yards.

Unless the boa constrictor had escaped from a zoo. That could be it. A gigantic snake had escaped from the local zoo, and it was under their tent!

Madison rolled over in her cot and peered at the tent floor. "I didn't see it."

Chloe gestured at the ground. "It was right there!"

"If you're trying to scare me, it isn't very funny," said Madison. "Well, it's *kind* of funny. A snake. What did it do, decide it needed a vacation from the snake shop?"

"Snake shop?" asked Avery.

"I meant pet store. They have snakes at pet stores sometimes."

"We're not trying to scare you," said Chloe. "There was something under the tent!"

"Then go out and see what it is."

"No! It could be a snake! We're not going outside the tent when there could be a snake crawling around out there!"

"Snakes don't crawl. They slither."

"Enough!" Chloe shouted. "You think I'm playing around, but I'm not. I know what I saw."

"I saw it too," said Avery. "And I felt it earlier."

Madison suddenly looked very scared. "You're not messing with me?"

"No!" the girls chorused.

"Then I'm going to call my mom. She can make sure the yard is clear, and then we can run inside the house."

Chloe wasn't ready to give up on the backyard campout, but she also didn't want to be dragged away by a giant python. They'd deal with the wildlife situation first, then worry about sleepover fun afterward. She watched the bottom of the tent carefully for any signs that the thing was still under there.

"Why aren't you calling?" Avery asked Madison.

Madison flashed the dark screen at Avery. "I'm waiting for my phone to turn on."

"Why did you turn it off?"

"I didn't!" Madison shook her phone, as if that would do anything. "The battery must be dead. It was fully charged. I charged it in the car on the way over."

Avery took her own phone out of her pajama pocket. "Hey, mine's off too." She held the side button and waited.

Chloe, who lost her phone on a regular basis, wasn't sure where she'd put hers.

"Mine won't turn on," said Avery a few seconds later.

"Are you kidding?" asked Chloe.

"Yes. It's a big funny prank. Madison and I worked it out while you were inside getting water. The snake puppet is working pretty well, isn't it?"

"You don't have to be sarcastic."

"I think I do." Avery held up her phone. "Seriously, it's not turning on."

Chloe looked around for her phone, almost hoping she

wouldn't be able to find it. If Avery and Madison had both drained their batteries, they could call it a coincidence—a huge one, but still a coincidence. If all three of their phones were dead, that was a sign of something very strange and serious.

Avery let out a yelp. "Something just moved past my leg!" She quickly scooted away.

"I think I saw it!" said Madison. She paused. "Can a snake chew through a tent?"

"Of course not," said Chloe. Then she wondered if that was true. *Could* a snake chew through a tent? She'd never heard of such a thing, but she'd also never been in a situation where she needed to know the gnawing habits of snakes.

There was no reason to panic. The snake, if it was even a snake, was not going to get into the tent. They needed to stay calm and not act like they were in a nightmare.

Avery began to shift items around: an extra sweatshirt, a packet of Twizzlers, her right shoe, then her left. Finally, she moved a pillow and found Chloe's phone. She pressed the button on the side. "Yours won't turn on either."

"Oh," said Chloe, because that seemed like a better answer than screaming.

What could possibly cause all three phones to have died?

Was there unusual electricity in the air? Were they suddenly trapped in the kind of horror movie where nobody's phones worked? *Was* this a nightmare?

Avery handed Chloe her phone. Chloe believed her best friend, but she tried to turn it on anyway, hoping the screen would light up and they could all have a good laugh about this.

The screen did not light up.

Chloe's breath caught in her throat. "It's all going to be fine," said Chloe, her voice sounding a bit too high. "There's got to be a logical explanation."

"Like what?" asked Avery.

"I don't know. If our phones worked, we could look it up."

"Maybe the snake knocked over the cell phone tower," Madison offered.

"Right," said Chloe. "Maybe the snake...no, that wouldn't explain why our phones won't even turn on."

"I was trying to be funny. I didn't really think a snake knocked over the tower."

"Oh. Of course. Sorry. Anyway, there has to be a reasonable answer. I don't know how my phone works, do you?"

"No," Avery admitted. "But when three of them stop working at the same time, and it's the same time that a giant snake is under the tent, something is really wrong."

"So, what should we do?" asked Madison.

The three girls looked at one another in the dim light.

Then, as if each of them realized what the others were thinking, they shouted, "*Mom!*" Even Avery, whose mother was not inside the house.

They shouted for their mothers for at least a full minute.

"How can they not hear us?" Chloe asked.

Avery shrugged. "Maybe they have the TV on really loud?"

They shouted some more, until Chloe's throat started to get sore.

Nobody came outside to investigate.

How was that possible? They weren't in a soundproof underground bunker. From inside their house, you could hear a car driving by or a dog barking down the block, so why couldn't Mom or Aunt Sandy hear them shouting?

"I'm scared," said Madison.

Chloe couldn't deny it—she was scared too. Something was under the tent, plus their phones were not working, *plus* nobody was answering when they shouted for help... There was something very deeply wrong. They might be in serious danger. Mom and Aunt Sandy might be in danger.

"Okay, let's think about this," Chloe said. "It could just be..."

She trailed off because she honestly had no idea what was happening. She could not explain any element of what was going on. Well, unless they really were in a nightmare. She pinched herself. It hurt. So much for "waking up" as a strategy.

"Maybe we're on a secret, scary reality show," said Madison. "Is my hair okay?" She straightened her pajamas.

"Really? Madison, I need you to try to focus right now," said Chloe. Yes, Chloe had also had a similar idea, but only for a fraction of a second as part of a series of thoughts that she quickly dismissed. She never would have said *maybe we're trapped in a horror movie* out loud.

Madison nodded. "I'll try," she promised.

"Thank you..."

"So, what could it just be?"

"Excuse me?" asked Chloe.

"You said, 'It could just be,' and then you trailed off. What could it just be?"

"I have absolutely no idea. None. Not a clue. Not even a theory."

"Oh," said Madison, sounding very disappointed.

"Maybe..." said Avery. She thought for a moment. "Maybe the snake is...never mind. Forget I said anything."

"Maybe the snake is what?" asked Chloe. Avery always had good ideas, although they were usually more about things to do when they were bored.

"I said to forget it."

"Maybe the snake is what? This could help us!"

"Magic."

"Okay," said Chloe. "I'm sorry I pried that out of you."

"It's all right."

Chloe looked around the tent. "You know what the snake *might* be?"

"What?" asked Madison.

"Gone. It hasn't come back since we've been talking about it. Maybe it slithered past us and went on its way."

"Except that—" Avery began.

"I know, I know," said Chloe. "It was here when we were setting up the tent earlier."

"Although you just felt a lump then. I *hope* it's the same thing."

"Yeah, I'll be really upset if we have to deal with both mysterious lumps and vicious snakes."

The girls were quiet for a moment.

"We should call for our moms again," said Madison. "Maybe they were watching the loud part in a movie."

Chloe, Avery, and Madison shouted at the top of their lungs. Screamed until they were out of breath. The entire neighborhood should have come running to find out what was wrong, but they didn't see or hear anybody investigating their distress calls.

Madison bit her lip. "Elijah wouldn't have gone to bed already, would he? How can *nobody* hear us?"

"We don't know that," said Chloe. "Someone might have called the police. You know, to help or to file a noise complaint."

"Maybe. So we...what, wait for the police to come?"

"Until we think of a better idea, yeah."

"How long does it take the police to respond?" asked Avery.

Chloe shrugged. "It can't be too long. What if the tent were on fire?"

"That would be the fire department."

"You know what I mean. If somebody called 911 about kids screaming, they aren't going to wait *too* long, right? They don't know what kind of danger we're in. It could be something way worse than being trapped in a tent by a snake. Let's wait. Somebody will come."

The girls waited silently.

"How long has it been?" asked Madison.

"I don't know," said Avery. "Our phones aren't working."

"A minute?"

"At least."

They continued waiting.

"I don't think anybody is coming to help us," said Chloe finally.

"Then what do we do?" asked Madison.

"We go for help ourselves. We're thirty steps from the house. We don't know if the snake is still out there. Let's make a run for it."

"All of us?"

"I'll do it," said Avery. "I'm the fastest."

"Since when?"

"Since always!"

"Fastest in your dreams, maybe," said Chloe.

"Do you want to race right—?"

"This isn't the time to argue," interrupted Madison.

"We're not really arguing," said Chloe. "We're joking around."

"This isn't the time to joke around."

"You were the one who said that thing about the snake knocking over the cell phone tower. Anyway, it doesn't matter." Chloe looked back at Avery. "We both run at the same speed, but it's my house, and I'm the reason we're out here. I'll go."

"I think I'm supposed to offer again to be polite, but I'm not going to," said Avery.

"I'll be fine," said Chloe. "The snake might not even be out there anymore. Besides, it might not attack me. If it does, it might not be venomous. If it is, please run inside and call an ambulance."

"If it coils around you, we'll pull it off," Avery promised.

"I appreciate that. So does everybody understand the plan?"

"You're going to make a run for it," said Madison.

"Right. Exactly. I'll unzip the flap to get out, and then you guys zip it back up. Go it?"

"Are you delaying because you're scared?" asked Avery.

"Yes. Very much so."

"I'll go."

Chloe shook her head. "No, no. I've got this. I should stop wasting time. There could be a second snake slithering around the yard." Suddenly she wished she hadn't mentioned a second snake. "I'm sure there's only one. Probably zero." She took a deep breath and let it out slowly.

"Everything will work out. It'll take me ten seconds to run inside, and then we'll find out that there's a logical explanation for everything that's happening, and then we'll never camp out in the backyard ever again."

"You're still stalling," said Avery.

Chloe unzipped the tent. She peered out, looking for a giant serpent waiting to attack her, but she couldn't see any movement in the grass. Or anywhere in the yard, really.

She took a moment to work up her courage.

"You should count 'three, two, one,'" said Madison.

"That's a good idea," Chloe agreed. She tensed, preparing to rush out of the tent to her back door. *"Three...two... one!"*

Chloe lunged out of the tent.

A tentacle burst through the lawn right in front of her.

CHAPTER 4

Chloe screamed.

The tentacle was almost as tall as she was. It looked like a cross between a tree branch and an octopus tentacle. It was dark brown, and though it didn't have suckers, it had scales and thorns. It was about as wide around as her bicep.

For a second, all she could do was stand there in horror.

Then she tried to move past the tentacle. It wrapped around her arm.

She screamed and tried to pull her arm free. The tentacle's grip was too tight.

Something—somebody—grabbed her other arm. Avery. Madison kicked the tentacle with her bare feet while Avery tried to yank Chloe free from it.

Chloe and Avery pulled so hard that Chloe thought her arm might pop right out of its socket.

Madison cried out in pain, the way you would if you kicked a tree with your bare feet. She might have also kicked one of the thorns.

"Help me pull!" said Avery.

Madison grabbed Chloe's arm as well, and the three of them tugged as hard as they possibly could.

"Your arm won't come free!" Avery shrieked at Chloe. This was not new information to Chloe, but in the terror of the moment, she didn't blame her friend for sharing unnecessary observations.

They continued pulling against the tentacle. Chloe was starting to believe her arm might literally come off, or at least her bones might pull free, leaving her with a skeletal appendage while her skin, muscle, and everything else remained in the tentacle's grip.

"Argh!" yelled Madison as she pulled.

"Just leave me!" Chloe wailed.

She was kind of proud of herself for being selfless. It was good to know that, in a crisis, her reaction wasn't, *Never leave me! If I die, we all die!*

"I'm not going to leave you!" yelled Avery.

Though she was feeling selfless, Chloe was glad to hear this.

"Madison!" Chloe shouted. "Run to the house while it's distracted!"

Madison let go of her arm and started toward the house. Another tentacle burst out of the ground, right in front of her.

She screamed again and tried to dodge the new tentacle, but it twisted to block her. The tentacle seemed to have gotten the same defense coaching as the girls did when playing soccer in phys ed: it shadowed the movements of her core; there was no way to pass.

Madison froze. The tentacle lunged toward her body, but she pulled away just in time.

Avery tried to dig her fingernails into the tentacle. Unfortunately, they weren't very long, and it didn't do any good.

Madison tried to maneuver past her tentacle again. It slapped her in the face. She let out a yelp of pain.

Chloe screamed one more time. At least she wasn't sobbing.

Avery leaned her head down, opened wide, and bit down on the tentacle.

Its grip on Chloe's arm loosened.

Chloe yanked her arm. It slid about an inch, but it didn't come free. She yanked again, and this time...it did!

As her arm popped free of the tentacle, Chloe lost her balance and fell back onto the grass.

Madison scrambled by her, back into the tent. Avery followed, and Chloe scooted backward, not taking her eyes off the two waving tentacles, until she was in the tent as well. She frantically zipped up the flap.

The three girls just sat there for a moment, trying to catch their breath.

"What *were* those things?" Avery asked.

"Why, they were obviously..." Chloe tried to think of something funny to say, but no jokes came to mind. "I have no idea."

"Is my face bleeding?" Madison asked, tentatively touching her cheek.

Chloe looked over at her. "No."

"It really hurts."

"There might be a mark on it, but it's not bleeding."

"Okay."

"I'm not going to lie," said Avery. "Now I wish it had been a snake."

"Where did they come from? What do we do?" asked Madison.

"I don't know," said Chloe. "We have to find a way to get back to the house. We don't know if we're safe here. But we don't know if there are two of those things or two thousand."

"Two is enough," groaned Madison.

"I barely got away from the one that grabbed me," said Chloe. "So I think until we have a plan, we stay in the tent."

"It didn't burst through the ground until you tried to leave," Avery pointed out.

Chloe nodded. "Maybe they aren't trying to hurt us. Maybe they're just trying to keep us here."

"Why would they do that?" asked Madison.

"I don't know! They're tentacles! I can't read their minds!"

"It's a good question, though," said Avery. "If we can figure out what they want from us, we might be able to figure out how to get away from them."

"Again, they're tentacles. They aren't going to give us a speech about their motives."

"Right, but we might be able to find it out based on what they do. You're the one who said that maybe they're trying to keep us in the tent."

"Don't argue," said Madison. "We need to work together."

"We do," Chloe agreed. "We definitely do. And we

already did. I really appreciate that neither of you left me behind to die."

"No problem," said Avery. "Think how awkward this would be right now if we had. What would we even talk about?"

"We'd have trouble making eye contact, that's for sure."

Avery nodded. "It would be, like, 'Hey, so when I pushed you aside and ran away screaming, that was to *help* you!'"

"We could have purposely sacrificed you to distract them," said Madison.

"Taking the joke too far, Madison," said Chloe.

"Sorry."

"Anyway, we might be safe for now. But I have absolutely no idea what's going on, and for whatever reason, those things don't seem to be trying to get into the tent, so…"

Something moved underneath the tent.

And then something else moved underneath the tent.

It slithered right beneath Chloe's foot.

"Get on my cot!" Madison shouted. She slid over on the pink cot and pulled up her legs to make room. Chloe and Avery scrambled up with her.

The cot was crowded with the three of them sitting on it, but at least it didn't feel like it was going to collapse.

Then Madison shifted her position a bit, and the cot wobbled.

"Nobody move," said Chloe.

They all sat there, trying to remain motionless.

With the sleeping bags on the floor, there was no way to tell if anything was moving underneath the tent. And Chloe really, really wanted to know if anything was moving underneath the tent. She carefully leaned over the side, grabbed the top of her sleeping bag, and tossed it so the bag folded in half. Then she did the same thing with Avery's sleeping bag.

It wasn't perfect, but it left about half the tent floor uncovered (excluding the part underneath the cot, which they couldn't see anyway).

Something slithered underneath the tent where Chloe's sleeping bag had been.

Followed by something else.

"I see three of them!" said Avery.

Chloe quickly glanced around, and, yes, three different lumps were moving under the vinyl.

"Don't panic," said Chloe. "They can't get us up here."

Chloe, of course, had absolutely no way of knowing if that was true. It almost definitely wasn't. But it seemed better than shouting, *We're doomed! We're doomed!*

The tentacles kept moving beneath the tent, like sharks under the ocean's surface.

"Maybe we should just run," said Avery.

Chloe shook her head. "The police could still come."

"Or our moms," added Madison.

"They haven't come yet."

"That doesn't mean they'll never come."

"I don't want to get killed by those things because we waited too long."

"I don't either, obviously," said Chloe. "But they aren't trying to get *in* the tent, and they *did* attack us when we left it. Think how much worse it could've been than my arm getting stretched and Madison getting slapped in the face."

Madison touched her cheek. "It still hurts."

"How do we know there aren't more and more of them gathering?" asked Avery.

"We don't," Chloe admitted. "But we don't even know what they are. Running for the house worked out really badly for us, and sitting here on this cot is working out much better."

"For now."

"Right, for now."

"I don't like the idea of waiting around until it's too late," said Avery.

"But we don't know that things are getting worse."

"They certainly aren't getting better," said Madison.

"Okay," said Chloe. "There are three of us. Let's take a vote. Should we stay here or try to make another run for it?"

"Are we actually voting, or are we asking Madison what she thinks, since she's the tiebreaker?"

"We're asking Madison."

"I don't know," said Madison.

"Well, *that's* helpful," said Chloe.

"I don't know what the best plan is! It was horrible out there. That thing could have gotten me in the eye. And Avery can't bite all of them."

"I'm not so sure about that," said Avery. She ran her tongue along the top of her teeth. "Although I think I chipped a tooth."

"I agree with Avery that maybe it's not smart to just sit here. But I also agree with Chloe that for all we know, help is on the way, and we're okay here for now."

"Thank you for that analysis," said Chloe. "But you're not really being a tiebreaker vote if you say both sides are right."

"I vote that we wait on the cot."

"Thank you."

Avery sighed. "She only said that because she's your cousin."

Madison shook her head. "No, I almost voted for your plan just so you wouldn't think I voted for Chloe because she's my cousin."

"I guess we wait then," said Avery. "Anybody know any good jokes?"

"Knock, knock," said Madison.

"I don't actually want to hear a joke," said Avery. "I was kidding."

"So, you were joking about wanting to hear a joke?"

"Please stop. If we all die, I don't want this to be our final conversation."

"We're not going to die," said Chloe. "We're going to be fine. I promise." Though she didn't know how.

"You can't promise that. It's a completely empty promise. For all we know, those things are going to rip through the tent five seconds from now."

The girls waited quietly for five seconds.

"See, you were wrong," said Chloe.

"I didn't say that they *were* going to rip through the tent.

I'm saying that if our plan is to sit here and do nothing, we need to consider what we want our last words to be."

"If you two live and I don't, tell people I said something really important and meaningful before I died," said Chloe.

"No," said Avery. "I'm going to tell them your final words were '*burrrrrrp*.'" She didn't actually belch when she said it, which was disappointing.

"That's only one word."

"I know. That makes it even worse." Avery pointed to the floor. "There's another one now."

"I only count three," said Chloe.

"I think one went under a sleeping bag or something."

Chloe sighed. "If you want to leave, we can leave."

"No, no, we took a vote, kind of." Avery shifted a bit. "If we make a run for it because I said to, and we all get torn apart by those things, I'll feel terrible."

"I think we'll be fine," said Chloe.

"You've gone from promising that we'll be fine to only thinking that we'll be fine."

"I promise we'll be fine," said Chloe, who honestly wasn't sure she even thought they'd be fine. They were all trying to carry on a lighthearted conversation, but she was absolutely terrified, and she knew Avery and Madison were too.

Who wouldn't be? What *were* those things?

"What if we starve to death?" asked Madison.

Chloe glared at her cousin. "Are you serious? We've been trapped here for five minutes. We just ate pizza and a million marshmallows. We're weeks away from starving to death. We'd die from thirst long before that, and those things might kill us before we died of thirst. Let's focus on our real problems."

"I'm sorry," said Madison. "I'm hungry."

"Even after all those marshmallows?"

"I feel like we're getting distracted," said Avery.

"Yeah," said Chloe. "But maybe it's good to be distracted and not have to think about those tentacles."

"What was that?" asked Madison.

"What?"

"That strange noise. It sounded like something under the cot."

The girls all stopped talking and listened.

"I don't hear anything," whispered Chloe.

"Maybe I imagined it."

And then Chloe heard it: a tearing sound.

"That's not good," she said. "That's really, really not good."

"Please tell me that's not the sound of something ripping through the tent," said Avery, her voice starting to shake.

"Maybe it's not."

The center of Chloe's sleeping bag lifted, like there was something in it.

"Oh no," she said. "No, no, no."

Another ripping noise came from under the tent.

"Everybody stay calm," said Chloe.

"Why should we stay calm?" asked Avery. "How does that benefit us?"

This time, the sound of vinyl tearing was accompanied by the sight of a tentacle bursting through the bottom of the tent. It rose almost to the ceiling and then bent in half, aiming directly at the girls, pointing accusingly at them.

Another tentacle burst through the bottom of the tent, inches from the cot.

Then one tore through the side, right next to the zipped-up door.

Another one ripped through the side. Then another. And another.

The girls screamed.

CHAPTER 5

One of the tentacles slid across the bottom of the tent, slicing it open from corner to corner.

Chloe screamed. Or at least she tried to scream. She was so scared that when she tried to open her mouth, nothing came out.

The girls scooted closer to one another on the cot. Madison was literally trembling with fear, which wasn't something Chloe had thought people actually did in real life.

"We...we need to get out of here," Avery whispered.

She was, of course, absolutely right. But Chloe was almost paralyzed with terror. She couldn't make herself move. She needed to move. She desperately needed to move. *Do something*, she screamed at herself inside her mind.

Another tentacle burst from the ground. This one,

thicker than the others, rose all the way to the top of the tent, lifting it.

The sides of the tent began to fully come apart.

For a moment, Chloe thought the entire tent was going to be carried away, leaving them completely exposed. But the tentacle tore through the top of the tent, and then it quickly sank back into the ground, as if something had yanked it down from underneath.

A tentacle—at least Chloe assumed it was a tentacle—struck the bottom of the cot.

This time Chloe was able to scream.

The tentacle struck the cot again and again. Then it coiled around the cot right between Avery and Chloe.

Both girls recoiled, trying to get away from it. The cot toppled over.

Chloe, Avery, and Madison spilled onto the ground. Chloe tried to cushion the fall with her hands. She landed directly on a tentacle with a hard thud.

It shrieked.

Well, no. The tentacle itself didn't shriek. Something under the tent shrieked. It let out a loud high-pitched wail that hurt Chloe's ears so badly, it made her cry out. Avery winced. Madison actually slapped her hands over her ears.

The wail lasted for a few seconds, and then the tentacle retracted into the ground.

"We can hurt them!" said Avery, getting to her feet.

Chloe and Madison also got up. Madison moved more slowly—Chloe hoped she hadn't injured herself in the fall.

"Help me with the cot!" Avery picked up one end of it. Chloe was baffled about why they'd want to pick up the cot, but she lifted the other end without questioning her friend.

"What are you doing?" asked Madison.

"Using it like a battering ram!"

Oh, of course. That made total sense. Chloe should have thought of that herself.

"Ready?" Avery asked Chloe.

Chloe nodded, even though she wasn't really ready. But if *sit on the cot and hope everything magically gets better* was a bad plan, *sit on the ground and hope not to be dragged away by the evil tentacles* was even worse.

They rushed forward, smacking tentacles out of the way with the cot as they did so.

Avery's plan seemed to have been that they'd run at the door flap and rip right through it. That was not what happened. Though the tentacles seemed to have no problem tearing through the tent material with their thorns, it was still a very well-made tent. The girls rammed into the door of the tent with the cot, and the entire tent toppled over. The trio tumbled forward as well.

Landing on the cot really hurt. Worse than the pain, though, was having the tent collapse on their heads. Chloe couldn't see what was happening around her!

She frantically felt around, trying to find the zipper.

A tentacle wrapped around her ankle.

She couldn't tug it free, so she began to slam her foot against the ground, as hard as she could.

It didn't let go. Her foot was bare, and she was slamming it against a grass lawn instead of concrete, so she probably wasn't hurting the tentacle much. She frantically felt for the zipper.

"I've got it!" said Madison. Chloe couldn't see what she was doing, but she heard her cousin unzip the tent.

"Let's go, let's go!" said Avery.

"One of them has me!"

"Not for long." Avery came into view as she stood up. "Madison, take an end."

Madison picked up the other end of the cot, and together they slammed it down upon the tentacle that was holding

Chloe. Another shriek reverberated around them, so piercing that Chloe thought her ears might bleed. But it let go.

Taking the cot with them, the girls emerged from the tent.

Chloe gulped fresh air into her lungs as they gazed out into the illuminated yard. At least they could see what they were facing. But there were now a dozen of them, so it wasn't as if she could relax and let out a sigh of relief.

"Run to your house!" shouted Avery.

It was a pretty obvious command, something they all would have come up with on their own, but it jolted everybody into action.

Madison grabbed the middle of the cot, and the three of them rushed toward the house.

A tentacle sprouted up in front of them, but they bashed into it with the cot and kept moving.

Madison cried out as a tentacle wrapped around her neck. It yanked her off her feet, then dragged her away with a muffled cry.

Avery let go of the cot. "Get in the house!" she told Chloe.

"We can't leave her!"

"We aren't! I'll help her while you run inside!" Without another word, Avery hurried off after Madison.

Chloe couldn't imagine leaving them behind, but Avery

was right—*somebody* needed to make it inside the house so they could call the police, or the military, or an exterminator, or whomever you'd call to deal with giant thorny tentacles popping up in your backyard.

She ran toward the back door.

A tentacle tripped her.

Chloe had two immediate thoughts as she landed face-first on the ground. Her first thought was that the fall had really hurt. Not the "landing on the lawn" part—though that didn't feel very good—but the part when she bit her tongue upon impact.

Her second thought was that she really didn't like that these tentacles were intelligent enough to purposely trip her. She didn't like that *at all*.

She pushed herself to her feet. Chloe knew she needed to focus on getting inside her house, but when Madison screamed behind her, she couldn't stop herself from turning around.

Avery was frantically trying to free Madison from the tentacle.

Chloe looked back at the door. There was a tentacle in the way, but only one, and if Chloe could just weave around it...

The door was only ten steps away. She could make it.

She bolted for the door, dodging the tentacle in front of her.

Another one burst up through the ground, so close that it scraped against her leg.

She dodged to the side.

The door to her house was *right there*. She'd get help! They'd be safe!

The tentacle lashed at her, the same way the other one had smacked Madison in the face. Chloe pulled her head back just in time.

She jolted toward the door again.

The tentacle jabbed her in the chest. It felt like somebody had punched her. She let out a grunt of pain and almost fell over again.

She forced herself to remain standing. She didn't want to die, and she also had a responsibility to Avery and Madison. Chloe was going to get help, no matter what.

The tentacle swung at her face.

She grabbed it before it could hit her, like she was in a superhero movie.

Chloe had brushed the other tentacle, the one she fell on in the tent, but she hadn't really noticed what it felt like. It was rough but damp, sort of like touching the bark of a tree after a heavy rain, and it had thorns, but not like a rosebush.

Nothing stabbed into her hands, but the tentacle gyrated and undulated like a snake.

She tried to bend it in half, as if to break it, but it folded over without seeming to be damaged.

Madison screamed again.

Chloe didn't look back. She held the tentacle between her hands and started toward the door again.

The tentacle jerked her backward.

She decided to use Avery's trick. She bit down on the tentacle, hoping it wouldn't break her teeth. After all this was over, she didn't want to have to go to the dentist too. But if she damaged her teeth trying to free herself, so be it.

Yuck. It tasted like licking a tree. She chomped off a bite and spit it on the ground.

The tentacle yanked out of her hands. But it didn't retract into the ground.

Once again, Chloe ran for the door.

She made it!

That same tentacle wrapped around her waist.

She grabbed the doorknob.

The tentacle pulled.

She tried to turn the knob, but her palm was too sweaty, and her hand slipped.

"Mom!" she shouted. "Mom, open the door! Open the door!"

She reached for the doorknob again, but the tentacle dragged her away, Chloe kicking and screaming the entire time.

"Let her go!" said Avery, who Chloe hadn't realized was right behind her. Avery and Madison grabbed the tentacle and tried to pry it away from Chloe's waist, even as it continued to drag her farther and farther away from the house.

Chloe wished she were wearing shoes. In her bare feet, there was no way to dig in her heels and gain ground.

Even with all three girls working together, Chloe was trapped.

Avery cursed in Spanish, then let go and ran off.

Chloe knew her friend wasn't abandoning her, but she was growing more frightened by the second.

"I need longer fingernails!" said Madison. Then she added, "And a manicure!"

Suddenly Chloe had a moment of clarity. This was *clearly* all a dream. Tentacles didn't just pop out of somebody's lawn. That was ridiculous. She had to be in the middle of a dream. Yes, it was extremely vivid, but when she woke up, she'd be back in the tent with a tummy ache from all the marshmallows.

She'd heard about this kind of dreaming—she couldn't remember the name of it—where you were aware that it was a dream and could control what was happening. Now that she'd figured out what was going on, she could sprout wings and fly away from all this.

Chloe imagined she had two graceful large wings...except she did not sprout wings and fly away.

And unless this was the most realistic dream anybody had ever had, she was indeed in her backyard being dragged from the safety of her home by a giant tentacle.

"Let go of her!" Madison shouted. The tentacle didn't listen.

Then Avery, who Chloe knew would never abandon her, was back. She had one of the marshmallow skewers in her hand.

"Try to stop moving!" Avery said.

Chloe did her best to still. Avery slammed the skewer into the tentacle like a spear. There was another earsplitting shriek, but Avery maintained her focus and stabbed the tentacle a few more times. Black ooze leaked from the skewer holes, which was less gross than it could have been.

The tentacle finally released its grip on Chloe and fell away.

"Go!" Avery shouted.

The girls ran toward the house again.

Two tentacles sprouted up in front of the door. Then two more. Then *three* more.

Fine. The girls veered toward the front yard as if they were of one mind.

Tentacles burst from the ground to block their way there as well.

Chloe wished Avery had collected more than one of the skewers. What else could they use to fight the tentacles?

Tent spikes!

She turned and ran for the remnants of the tent. She didn't say what she was doing, just in case the tentacles could hear and understand her. It would be really weird if they could, but she didn't want to take any chances.

She crouched and grabbed the top of a spike. She yanked on it.

It wouldn't come out of the ground. Apparently they'd pounded it in too well—it had been the only easy part about putting up the tent!

Chloe grimaced with effort, but she didn't stop.

A new tentacle burst out of the ground right next to her hands.

"Seriously?!" Chloe yelled. "Back off!"

CHAPTER 6

Chloe was not happy to see the tentacle, but its sudden appearance had loosened the dirt around the tent spike, and Chloe was able to yank it out of the ground.

Avery jabbed the marshmallow skewer into the tentacle. Whatever shrieked under the lawn was starting to numb Chloe's hearing. It was just as loud, but not as painful.

Madison also held a tent spike. She was better than Chloe at pulling tent stakes out of the lawn, a skill Chloe had never really thought much about before today. Madison swung the spike at one of the tentacles and missed.

Chloe looked back at the house. Though the door wasn't *completely* blocked—she could see bits of the wood behind the writhing creatures—it was pretty close. If they'd had an axe or a chain saw, maybe they could've gotten through the wall of tentacles, but she didn't think two tent spikes and a marshmallow skewer were going to do the trick.

"We aren't going to be able to fight our way through them!" yelled Chloe.

"What about the tree house?" asked Madison.

Avery shook her head. "I don't want to get trapped up there."

"I don't want to get trapped up there either," said Chloe. "But I also don't want to die down here."

"We're not going to die," said Avery with determination. "We won't let that happen."

"Not sure how much say we have in that."

"We have a *lot* of say in it."

Every second they stood there discussing the situation was time they weren't moving to safety, so they really needed to decide.

"They've completely barricaded the door!" said Chloe. She didn't want to be Ms. Negative, but they also had to accept reality.

Avery hurried over to the cot. "C'mon! We still have our battering ram!"

Chloe didn't want to fight her way through the tentacles with a cot and some tent spikes, but the tree house would be a dangerous place even if the backyard *weren't* overtaken by some alien-like creature. Avery was right. They had to keep trying to get inside the house.

Chloe and Avery each picked up an end of the cot. It was better than nothing, Chloe supposed, though awkward to carry while they were still trying to hold the skewer and spike.

They ran toward the door.

Chloe couldn't help but think this would be easier if they had a golf club or a bat to swing, striking tentacles out of their way as they ran. And she was good at Whac-A-Mole when the carnival came to town each summer. They couldn't really swing the cot, so all they could do was plow into their enemy and hope that it would retreat.

They smacked into a tentacle. It retracted into the ground.

Another one ducked underneath the cot. Did it count as "ducking" if it was a tentacle? Chloe wasn't sure, but that was what it did.

They were almost to the door!

"Just smash right into them!" Avery shouted.

Chloe ran even faster, hoping she wouldn't break her arms when they struck their target.

The tentacles, all seven of them moving at the exact same time, dodged the cot. Chloe and Avery ran into the door, hard, and Chloe bit her tongue again. They stumbled backward from the impact but kept their grip on the cot.

The tentacles twisted together, like they were braiding themselves. Within a couple of seconds, they'd become one large tentacle.

The giant tentacle whipped upward, knocking the cot out of their hands. It flew into the air, and Chloe and Avery rushed along the side of the house to avoid being hit by it when it crashed back down.

Madison stepped between them dramatically, like she was making a grand entrance, and jammed her tent spike into the tentacle, burying it completely in the creature. Once again, something under the ground screeched. It was louder than before.

All three girls had to cover their ears. The sound was so piercing that Chloe could feel it rattle her teeth.

The tentacle braid thing wrapped around Madison's feet and lifted her upside down into the air.

"Let her go!" Chloe screamed. She felt kind of silly, because the tentacle almost certainly couldn't hear her or understand her. It wasn't likely to shrug and reply, *Oh my. Well, if I'm going to get shouted at, so I suppose I should let her go. Sorry for the inconvenience, ma'am.*

Technically, the tentacle did let Madison go. But it did so by flinging her across the yard. She screamed the entire way before landing about twenty feet from the back door. When she hit the ground, she went immediately silent.

Chloe didn't have time to process her horror before the tentacle wrapped around Avery's feet. She jabbed her marshmallow skewer at it but lost her grip on the weapon as the tentacle dangled her upside down, the same way it had Madison.

Chloe grabbed her friend's hands.

The tentacle tried to tug Avery away from her, but Chloe refused to let go. She pulled as hard as she possibly could. Avery winced in pain as Chloe and the tentacle yanked her in opposite directions.

Chloe tried to brace herself. Her bare feet slid across the grass as the tentacle continued pulling her friend away from her.

"Don't let go!" Chloe shrieked.

Avery popped out of her grasp.

The tentacle flung her across the yard. She landed with a thump right next to Madison, close enough that it jostled her body.

Don't get distracted, Chloe told herself. *They're fine. They have to be.*

She went on the offensive, stabbing at the tentacle, again and again, before it could grab her. She forced herself to ignore the ground-shaking shrieks.

Black ooze trickled out of the tentacles' wounds.

One of the tentacles unraveled itself from the others and slapped her arm. It stung, but Chloe didn't release her grip on the tent spike. Then it wrapped around her wrist and yanked her hand up toward her head, as if trying to make her jab herself in the face.

She let go of the spike just in time. She punched herself.

Yeow!

Her vision went blurry for a moment, but she had to stay focused. She could worry about how much everything hurt later. She had to survive and help her friends.

Though she'd lost her weapon, she still had her teeth. She opened wide. The tentacle yanked out of the way before she could chomp down upon it. She tried a few times, but it kept dodging her, avoiding her jaws.

Then it made her punch herself again. Lightly. Playfully.

Chloe couldn't help but think the creature was trying to be...funny but cruel. Like a school bully.

She really wished that Avery and Madison would shout something at her so she'd know they were okay.

The other six tentacles, still braided together, wrapped around Chloe's ankles. They yanked her into the air, lifting her so that her head dangled above the grass, her hair brushing the tips of the lawn.

Instead of flinging her away like it had done with Avery and Madison, it just held her there.

She felt like it was studying her.

Not that it had any eyes, as far as she could tell.

Of course, the tentacles could use other senses. Maybe even sonar like a bat or whatever.

The blood rushed to her head.

"Put me down!"

The tentacle didn't move.

Chloe had a horrifying thought: What if instead of letting her go, the thing slammed her into the ground, over and over and over and over, like something from a bad cartoon, until all her stuffing came out?

She struggled and twisted, trying to get loose. The tentacle's grip was too firm.

"Chloe!" Madison shouted.

Chloe looked over. Madison was back on her feet and helping Avery up. They were okay!

The tentacles tossed Chloe across the yard. For a moment,

she was flying. Chloe flailed her arms. She wasn't just on a collision course with the ground—she was going to hit Avery!

Maybe Avery would move out of the way in time. Maybe Chloe would land on an unusually cushy spot on the ground. If not, one or both of them were going to collide painfully in the next couple of seconds.

Instead of moving out of the way, Avery and Madison held out their arms, attempting to catch her.

And they did...kind of.

She landed on them, and all three girls fell to the ground in a heap.

They lay there for about five seconds, which was long enough for Chloe to determine that she hadn't broken any bones, at least not any important ones. Then the three girls helped one another up.

The tentacles hovered at a distance, as if assessing their next move.

"Should we try again?" asked Madison.

Their weapons had been kind of pathetic, and they didn't even have those anymore. Though Chloe didn't want to be a whiner, right now she really felt like whining. She would go along with whatever plan Avery had in mind, but she hoped someone had another idea.

Avery looked over at the house and sighed. "I don't know."

Chloe's stomach flip-flopped. She didn't like hearing that. Whether it was for what movie they should watch, what toppings to get on a pizza, or what they should do when tentacles burst into their tent, Avery always had a plan.

"I'm not sure I can run," Madison admitted. "My leg really hurts."

Chloe looked toward Elijah's house. There were no tentacles in Elijah's yard.

"You see that?" she asked.

"What?" asked Avery.

Chloe pointed. There were a few tentacles in the way, but not a single one in his yard. Of course, that didn't mean some wouldn't sprout up if they ran over there...

"Run!" Avery shouted.

Chloe slung an arm around Madison, and together they all sprinted toward Elijah's yard. Several tentacles popped up at the edge of Chloe's lawn, creating a barricade as if they knew what the girls were trying to do.

Chloe spun around. The path to her back door was clear, but she was sure they'd return if they tried that plan again.

"What about the tree house?" asked Madison.

Avery shook her head. "It's rickety. Sorry, Chloe. I know your dad worked hard to build it, but I don't want to get trapped up there."

"Okay," said Chloe.

Avery glanced around the yard, seemingly assessing their predicament. "On second thought, maybe that's not a bad idea."

"Are you sure?" asked Chloe.

"No," said Avery. "I'm very much not sure. But the tentacles aren't much taller than we are, so the tree house might be out of their reach."

"Let's do it," said Chloe.

They all ran for the tree house. A tentacle popped up in front of them because tentacles were *always* popping up in front of them, but Avery angrily grabbed it with both hands. She squeezed.

"What are you trying to do?" asked Chloe. "Strangle it?"

"Tear it out of the ground!"

"No! Get to the tree house!"

"Help Madison while I distract it! I'll be right behind you!" Avery shouted.

Chloe hoped her friend was okay. Obviously, none of them were okay, but Avery seemed to be a lot more frightened and disoriented than she had been before the tentacles flung her across the backyard.

Yet there was no time to be afraid. They had to get to the tree house.

CHAPTER
7

Chloe assumed a million things would go wrong while they tried to climb into the tree house, so she was surprised to make it up there without any problem. Oh, the rickety ladder had jiggled, but her foot hadn't broken through any of the rungs, and the floor of the tree house didn't collapse when she stepped inside. Honestly, it wouldn't have shocked her if the entire thing had disintegrated into sawdust or at least come loose from the tree and crashed to the ground. They weren't having the best of luck that night.

She helped Madison up, and Avery made it into the tree house right after.

They were safe!

Maybe.

Temporarily.

They were about twelve feet in the air. The tentacles were only about half that height. Of course, they didn't know how far they *could* stretch, but maybe the girls were out of reach up here. That would be nice. Chloe was getting really tired of those things.

The tree house floor was covered with dust and leaves, and the red paint had almost completely faded away. Otherwise, it was just as she'd left it over a year ago: A couple of dolls. Some empty soda cans. A sketchbook in which she'd done some not-great drawings. Oh, and there was Avery's light-green jacket that she hadn't been able to find. Chloe wondered why *maybe we left it up in the tree house* hadn't occurred to either of them. She'd probably outgrown it by now.

There was one new addition to the furnishings: a very large wasp's nest in the upper-left corner. Chloe didn't see any wasps circling it, so she hoped it was empty.

They all peered over the side railing. The tentacles were still there—at least twenty of them poking out of the yard—but there weren't any near the tree house, though their movement had left a few holes near the tree.

"Are we safe?" Madison asked.

Chloe shrugged. "Safer than we were."

"I'll take it." Madison looked around. "Is there any food up here?"

"Nobody's been up here in a year, Madison."

"I wasn't asking for a carton of milk. Maybe a box of Twinkies?"

"No Twinkies, sorry."

"What about water?"

"We aren't going to be up here long enough to worry about food and water."

"Are you sure?" Madison asked.

Chloe had to admit that, no, she was not sure. She couldn't imagine that they'd be trapped up here past morning, though. Mom and Aunt Sandy hadn't heard their shouting, but they weren't living out in the middle of the forest. They had plenty of neighbors. *Somebody* would come. Or their mothers would come looking for them in the morning. They were big proponents of a healthy breakfast.

Avery took her phone out of her pajamas pocket. She pressed the side button and waited for it to turn on. All three girls stared at the screen, holding their breath.

The phone didn't turn on.

Avery sighed. "Worth a try."

"Yep," said Chloe. "I wish we had flares, or bottle rockets, or anything we could use to get somebody's attention."

"I wish we had a portable jet pack to fly out of here," said Avery.

"I wish we had a flamethrower," said Madison. "I bet those things wouldn't put up much of a fight against a flamethrower."

"Oh, yeah, I like that idea," said Chloe. "I'd much rather have a flamethrower than a bottle rocket."

"I wish we had a kitten," added Avery. "Everything is nicer when you have a purring kitten on your lap."

"I wish we had a monkey to distract us from our problems," said Madison. "You can never be sad and scared when there's a monkey around."

Chloe laughed. It felt good to think about something else.

Then, of course, she remembered their situation.

"I don't think there are as many of them out there," she said.

Avery and Madison looked. "You're right," said Avery. "A few of them are gone. I wonder why?"

"Maybe we outsmarted them and they've moved on."

Chloe watched as one of the tentacles withdrew into the ground.

"Do you think they're retreating?" asked Madison.

"No," said Avery. "They're probably just conserving energy. No reason to be flailing around the yard if we're up here."

"It's good, though," said Chloe. "If they could reach us, they'd be trying, right? They wouldn't just go back under the ground."

Avery nodded. "I think you're right. They can't get us up here." She leaned a bit out of the tree house and shouted, "Sorry to *disappoint* you!"

"So we wait?" asked Madison.

"Sure, why not?" said Avery. "If this tree house doesn't fall apart before morning, we'll be fine."

"If morning comes," said Madison dramatically.

"Why would you say that?" asked Chloe.

"I dunno," said Madison. "It was just something that occurred to me to say."

"Well, don't. We're finally safe, so please don't talk about how the sun is never going to rise again."

"That's not at all what I said. I said 'if morning comes'..."

"It's the same thing."

"It sounds way more grim the way you said it. And I said '*if.*' I never said morning *wasn't* going to come. I'm pretty sure morning *is* going to come. So there."

"Why would you bring something like that up in the first place?" asked Chloe.

"Our phones don't work," said Madison. "Our mothers can't seem to hear us screaming. Giant monster tentacles have infested your backyard. I don't think it's that big of a stretch to wonder if the sun will ever rise again."

"See, now you're saying it in the grim way," said Chloe.

"Knock it off, both of you," said Avery.

"I'm not doing anything wrong!" Madison insisted. "What if it's the end of the world? Why shouldn't we talk about that? Why do we have to sit here and pretend everything is fine?"

"Because it's *not* the end of the world," said Chloe. "And because, after what we just went through, I'd like to have two minutes to catch my breath before I start worrying about the next big problem. Which is not the end of the world, because it's not."

"Right," said Avery.

"What?" asked Chloe.

Avery gave her a confused frown. "Huh?"

"Why did you say it like that?"

"Why did I say what like that?"

"You said 'right' like you didn't believe it."

"No, I didn't."

"Yes, you did," insisted Chloe. "Do you think it's apocalypse too?"

"No. I mean...no. No, of course it's not. We have absolutely no reason to believe this is the end of the world. It could simply be an alien invasion."

"I hadn't thought of that," said Madison. "The tentacles could be aliens whose technology is blocking our phones' signals and creating some kind of invisible force field that's keeping our moms from hearing us."

"Seriously? That's ridiculous," said Chloe. She paused. "Okay, no, it's not. It actually makes a lot of sense. It could be aliens. Honestly, I hope it is. I'd much rather it be aliens than the end of the world."

"Aliens could bring about the end of the world," Madison pointed out. "I mean our world, not theirs."

Chloe shook her head. "Please stop talking. You're not helping."

"Hey, we're having a conversation. That's impressive, considering. We could be screaming, and crying, and tearing out our hair. And we're not. That's pretty good, don't you think?"

"It is," said Avery.

"Then hooray for us," said Chloe. "But we could spend less time talking about it being the end of the world and more time trying to figure out how to get out of this."

Avery admitted, "I thought we were waiting to be rescued."

"Me too," said Madison.

"I mean, I wouldn't have climbed up the tree if I thought we needed a plan for how to get out of it too," said Avery.

"Fine," said Chloe. "But what happens if...?"

"The sun doesn't rise?" asked Madison.

"No!"

"If the sun does rise, but we're still trapped in this void where our phones don't work and nobody can hear us?"

"I meant more like...I don't know, if the tree house falls apart," said Chloe. "What will we do if the tree house falls apart?"

"Climb farther up the tree and sit on a branch," suggested Avery.

"Good!" said Chloe. "That's good! Now we have a plan. See how much better that is than talking about being trapped in eternal darkness?"

"Also, if the tree house breaks, we can use some of the boards as weapons," added Madison.

"Right!" said Chloe. "We sure can! And some of these boards will have nails in them. See, that's way more productive than talking about whether or not the sun will come up."

"I think you're way more worried about the sun than the rest of us," said Avery.

"I wasn't! But then Madison put it in my head!"

"Sorry," said Madison.

Chloe looked back down at the ground. "And here's one more thing we should be talking about. Most of the tentacles are gone." She pointed, even though Madison and Avery obviously knew where to look. There were only four left.

And then three.

"That's great!" said Madison.

"We made it," said Chloe. "Did the tent get ruined? Yeah. That's a bummer, but we can always get a new one."

"We have a tent at home you can borrow," said Madison. "It has a separate little room in the front."

For once, Chloe was grateful to her cousin. "See? Problem solved. I don't think I'd roast marshmallows on that skewer again, but we can get a new one when we go shopping for a tent." Chloe forced herself to smile. She was still scared—terrified, really—but unless one of those tentacles stretched up to grab them, the girls seemed to be safe.

Chloe didn't believe this was the end of the world. It was just a really bizarre event.

"Should we try to sleep in shifts?" Madison asked. "I volunteer to take the first watch."

"There is no way I'm getting any sleep," said Chloe. "I wouldn't be able to sleep up here even without the monsters down there."

"Me neither," said Avery. "This tree house is kind of lopsided. I'd be worried that if I fell asleep, I'd roll right out. But, Madison, if you want to sleep, we'll keep an eye out and wake you if there's any danger."

"Oh, I'd never be able to sleep," said Madison. "That's why I offered to take the first shift. I was just trying to be nice in case either of you was tired."

"I may never sleep again," said Chloe.

Another tentacle quietly retracted into the ground.

"Only two left," said Avery. "Maybe they got bored."

"That would be nice."

"Do you mind if I try an experiment?"

"What kind of experiment?" Chloe asked.

Avery picked up one of the aluminum cans and hurled it onto the lawn. A tentacle immediately popped up next to it and grabbed it.

"Not the result I was hoping for," she said.

"It's okay," said Chloe. "As long as they aren't trying to climb the tree, we're fine." She wasn't sure she believed that, but she might as well be optimistic.

Then she heard a creak that sounded very much like a screen door opening.

But not hers—next door.

"It's Elijah!" she said.

CHAPTER 8

They watched as Elijah crept out of the back door of his house and then carefully shut the door behind him.

"Elijah!" Chloe shouted. "Hey, Elijah!"

He looked into Chloe's yard and smiled.

"Elijah!" Avery screamed. "We're up in the tree house!"

Elijah gave no indication that he heard them. He put on a werewolf mask and slowly creeped toward Chloe's yard.

"He's trying to scare us," said Madison.

"What is he seeing?" asked Chloe. "Can't he tell that the tent is destroyed and the yard is a disaster?" There were still three tentacles hovering, including the one Avery had drawn out with the can. Why didn't he notice them?

Then Elijah stopped.

Crouched.

Tied his shoes.

"Elijah!" Chloe shouted, as loud as she possibly could. She couldn't *not* try to get his attention.

"What do we do?" asked Madison.

Chloe had no idea. She couldn't let him walk to his doom, but how could they warn him if he couldn't see or hear them? Was she about to watch her neighbor die?

Elijah stood back up and adjusted the mask. If she weren't so worried about his safety, she'd be mad that he was trying to ruin their campout.

He resumed walking toward her yard.

Chloe, Avery, and Madison watched in silent horror.

As soon as Elijah crossed the property line, he stopped. Tilted his head. He took off the mask, and it slid out of his hand to the ground.

"Chloe?" he called out, fear ringing in his voice. "Chloe, what—what's—?"

A dozen tentacles sprouted up all at once.

All three girls shouted his name.

He looked up at the tree house.

A tentacle wrapped around his foot.

Oh no! Had they distracted him?

Elijah just stood there, looking completely panicked. Chloe

couldn't blame him. He'd thought he was playing a prank, only to become a guest in Chloe Whitting's Yard of Horrors.

The tentacle yanked him off his feet. He landed on his side. He cried out.

Chloe needed to be more like Avery: a girl with a plan. She couldn't stand there watching. She had to get down there and save him!

Madison had already had the same idea. Before Chloe could move, Madison had hurried over to the ladder and was climbing down.

Somebody needed to help Elijah, but Madison was not the fastest or most physically fit of the three. She was always asking to sit out in gym class, and she'd hurt her leg earlier, after all. Yes, she was the one who least wanted to see Elijah get dragged away by the creature in the yard, but no matter how annoying he was, *none* of them wanted to see that.

But it was too late. Madison was already halfway down the ladder.

Elijah tried desperately to pull his leg away from the tentacle, but he couldn't free himself.

Madison *almost* made it to the ground before one of the ladder rungs broke. She was two rungs from the bottom when it split in two. She cried out in surprise and fell.

Fortunately, it wasn't very far, and she didn't appear to have been more injured. Since she'd been flung across the lawn, Chloe supposed that falling part of the way off a ladder was no big deal in comparison.

A tentacle slithered around Elijah's arm. He let out a scream that would've been amusing under other circumstances. The tentacle around his arm and the one around his foot began to pull in opposite directions...

...as if they were trying to rip him in half!

"Help me!" Elijah wailed.

One half of the broken rung had come off completely, so Madison picked it up and ran to Elijah.

He bellowed in pain. Chloe watched in horror as the tentacles continued to pull him. Would his arm pop off? Would his leg? Would he rip in two at the belly?

His body rose a few inches off the ground as the tentacles pulled tighter and tighter.

Madison crouched and smashed the ladder rung into the tentacle that held Elijah's leg. It didn't budge. She adjusted the rung in her hands, then slammed it into the tentacle again. It still didn't let go, but that awful screech sounded from beneath the ground. Elijah slapped his free hand over his ear.

Madison kept stabbing the tentacle with the wood. The

black ooze was getting all over her pajamas, but she was determined.

Finally, the tentacle retracted into the ground, and Elijah dropped back onto the lawn.

Without hesitation, Madison crawled over to Elijah's arm and continued the tentacle-stabbing process. She was getting pretty good at it. This tentacle also retracted, freeing Elijah.

For now.

Madison stood, then reached for Elijah. "C'mon!"

"What's happening?"

"Bad stuff. Let's go."

Elijah took her hand, and she helped him to his feet. He looked around the yard, gaping at the tentacles. "They're everywhere!" he cried out.

"There are fewer than there were earlier," Madison assured him, though Elijah didn't seem particularly reassured. She tugged on his arm, and they ran for the tree house.

She screamed as a tentacle wrapped around her leg.

Elijah stomped on it. Unlike the girls, he was wearing shoes, so this was a lot more effective. Another screech, and the tentacle let her go.

Madison quickly climbed the ladder.

Elijah followed.

The nearest rung broke beneath his feet. He pulled himself up to the next rung, which also broke.

"Not so hard!" Avery shouted.

A tentacle slithered up the ladder toward his legs.

Elijah looked up at the girls. "I'm gonna fall!"

"Don't fall!" said Chloe unhelpfully.

Elijah pulled himself up farther. He was still out of the girls' reach. He braced his feet against another rung, and it broke as well.

"Stop breaking the ladder!" Avery shouted.

"It's not my fault!"

"Be gentle!"

"I'm trying to hurry!" Elijah looked down. "It's trying to get me!"

"Stop looking down!"

"I can't!"

"Stop it!"

"I can't!"

"Keep climbing!"

"I don't wanna die!"

"Then keep climbing!"

Elijah kept going, breaking two more rungs of the ladder as he did so. Chloe and Avery reached down, grabbed his arms, and pulled him onto the platform. He immediately scurried to the middle of the tree house, whimpering.

"Don't you wish you hadn't tried to scare us?" asked Chloe.

"What *are* those things?"

"Tentacles."

"But *whose* tentacles?"

Chloe shrugged. "We don't know."

"Where did they come from?"

"You're asking a lot of questions that we don't know the answers to."

"But where did they come from?"

"Elijah..."

"Be nice to him," said Madison. "He just went through something really scary."

"We've been going through something scary all night!" said Chloe.

"Right. We've had time to get used to it."

"You're *used* to it?"

"Have you called the police?" asked Elijah.

"Our phones don't work," replied Madison.

"Why don't your phones work?"

"We don't know."

"Does *my* phone work?"

"Try it."

Elijah took his phone out of his pocket. "It turned off." He pressed a button and waited. "It won't turn on."

"Then we have our answer," said Chloe.

"Are they still down there?" asked Elijah, panic still in his voice. "Can they get us up here?"

"Yes, they're still down there. We don't know if they can get us up here. They haven't tried, so we think we're safe."

"I don't feel safe."

"Just take a deep breath," said Avery. "Think about puppies. That helped us."

"I'm thinking about puppies with tentacles!"

"Then don't think about puppies."

Elijah closed his eyes, took a few deep breaths, then opened his eyes again. "I'm better now."

"If you need to suck your thumb, it's okay," said Chloe, trying to make a joke, but no one laughed.

"I'm not freaking out anymore. I just wasn't expecting this."

"No one would," said Avery.

"It was so weird. I thought it would be funny to scare you, so I got my favorite werewolf mask and snuck out. I was going to scrape my fingers along the tent, like they were werewolf claws. Then you would've come out to investigate, and I'd be there looking like a werewolf, and it would've been great."

"We wouldn't have thought you were a real werewolf," said Chloe.

"But still..."

"It would've been funny," Madison offered with a little smile at Elijah.

"So then I..." Elijah trailed off. "You won't believe me."

"Seriously?" asked Chloe. "After what just happened, you think we won't believe you? Do you remember that time when you walked into my yard and almost got ripped in half by a creature's tentacles? Try us."

Elijah continued, ignoring her sarcasm. "I walked outside. Everything looked totally normal. I could see your tent. It was right where it had been before, and it was all in one piece. I could see lights inside it like you were all on your cell phones. But the second I stepped into your yard, everything changed. Suddenly your tent was shredded and pieces were scattered all over, and those...*things* were popping out of the ground, and you were all screaming at me. I thought I was having a nightmare."

"It's pretty close to one," said Avery.

"I'm sorry I panicked. I think that if I'd seen the messed-up tent and the tentacles from my yard, I would've had time to figure things out, but having it all appear at once like it was a magic trick was too much."

"Right," said Chloe. "I'm sure you would have been very, very brave."

"Be nice, Chloe."

Since that had come from Avery and not Madison, Chloe nodded. "I'm sorry. We're all really stressed out."

"*Yeah*, we are," said Elijah. "Now what?"

"We're glad you're here," said Madison.

"Well, no. We're not," said Avery. "Our ladder is broken."

"That's not a big deal, though," said Madison.

"Actually, yeah, it kind of is, if we want to get down from here. And before, Elijah was safe in his house, and now he's in serious danger, so you shouldn't be *too* glad he's here."

"It's okay," said Elijah. "I know what she meant. Thanks, Madison."

"You two better not kiss," said Chloe with a harrumph.

Elijah and Madison both laughed, then looked embarrassed.

"So what's the plan?" asked Elijah.

"There isn't one," said Chloe.

"We should have a plan. Plans are good in times like this."

"We do have a plan," said Avery. "The plan is to wait up here. It's safe, as far as we know. We'll wait until morning, and then somebody will see us up here and..." She frowned. "Oh. I guess they won't."

"Let's not panic," said Madison. "We don't know that everybody will see things the way Elijah did."

"No, but it would explain why your moms didn't hear us. I bet that even if they peek outside to check on us, it'll look like everything is completely normal. For all we know, we could be up here for weeks, and everybody will think we're lounging in the tent, telling ghost stories."

Chloe shook her head. "Even if my mom or Aunt Sandy don't check on us tonight, they will in the morning. They aren't going to simply forget about us. Elijah didn't."

"Right," said Elijah. "It's not like I forgot you existed."

"We appreciate you not forgetting that we existed," Madison told him. "Is time passing at a normal rate for you?"

"Huh?"

"Nothing strange going on with time? Chloe was concerned that the sun might never rise again, and that would probably have something to do with time stopping, so I wanted to make sure time was fine when you came out here."

"Oh, yeah, time was fine, no problems there," said Elijah. "Of course, I wasn't in your yard. Maybe that's not the case anymore."

"Oh no," said Chloe.

"Let's not worry about that now," said Avery. "We'll have plenty of..."

"What?" asked Chloe.

"Nothing."

"You were going to say that we'll have plenty of *time* to worry about *time* later, weren't you?"

"Yes, but I caught myself..."

"Caught yourself in time?" Chloe couldn't help it. She cracked herself up.

"Enough." Avery looked over at Elijah. "When we sent you away the first time, about how long was it before you came back?"

"About an hour, maybe."

"That's about how long it was for us too. Good. Let's worry about the tentacles."

"Also, there's a big wasp's nest up here," said Elijah. "Did you all notice that?"

"Yes," said Chloe. "Don't touch it."

"Anyway," said Avery, "if time is passing normally, somebody will come outside to check on us in the morning."

"And then get attacked by those things," said Elijah.

"Oh no," said Madison.

"Yes, but they'll be right there at the door," said Avery. "Your mom or Chloe's mom will open the door, a tentacle will try to grab her, and she'll go right back inside and call the police. They'll send somebody to investigate, call in the fire department, maybe. It'll all work out. All we have to do stay in the tree house."

"We should be able to handle that," said Chloe.

"If you want to sleep in shifts, I'll take the first watch," offered Elijah.

"Nobody is sleeping," said Avery.

"Okay, just trying to be polite."

"Are the tentacles still out there?" Madison asked.

Chloe looked out onto the yard. "They're...oh. *Oh*. Oh no..."

CHAPTER 9

Elijah remained seated, but Avery and Madison scooted to the edge to see what Chloe was talking about.

"Oh, yeah," said Avery. "That's *no bueno*."

"Super *no bueno*," Chloe agreed.

Several tentacles were wrapped around the tree trunk.

"What are they doing?" asked Madison.

"Maybe they're giving the tree a hug to show how much they love it," said Avery.

"Seriously, what are they doing?"

"I don't want to be all doom and gloom," said Chloe, "but if I had to guess, I'd say they're trying to pull down the tree."

"Can they do that?"

"You have the same amount of information that I do, Madison."

"Okay, well, it's not like the tree is shaking."

Everybody was quiet for a moment.

"Did the tree just wiggle?" asked Madison.

"No," said Chloe.

"Are you sure? I felt something."

"You're imagining it."

"Why would I imagine it?"

"Because we just talked about the tree moving!"

Madison sat motionless for a few seconds. "Maybe I did imagine it. I hope so."

"There's no reason to think they can pull down an entire tree," said Chloe, even though there were *plenty* of reasons to think they could. This wasn't some gigantic oak tree that had been growing for hundreds of years. It was a regular-sized tree, one that was probably a little small to support a tree house.

Another tentacle emerged from the ground, then slithered up the base of the tree before stopping near where the third rung of the ladder had been.

What was it doing?

It seemed to be straining.

A broken tree root burst out of the ground.

"They're trying to tear up the roots!" shouted Chloe.

"How bad is that?" Madison asked.

"It's not great."

"Should we flee the tree?"

Avery giggled.

"What?"

"Sorry. Flee the tree. It rhymes."

"And...?" Madison asked.

"I got two seconds of joy out of your accidental rhyme. Now we can move on."

"I think it's too soon to try to escape the tree house," said Chloe. "Pulling at some roots doesn't mean they'll be able to bring the whole tree down. Until the tree starts to feel wobbly, we're safer up here than trying to make a break for my house or Elijah's. But that's just my opinion. Everybody gets a say. Except Elijah. We can put it to a vote."

"Why don't I get a say?" asked Elijah.

"Because you were late."

"I saved you! No, wait. Madison saved me. Anyway, I don't want a vote. I'm happy to have other people make the decision. But do you think my yard is safe?"

"I don't know," said Chloe. "It might be."

"I had no idea what was happening over here until I stepped onto your property. Maybe they don't have any power outside your yard. If we can get into my yard, maybe none of this will be a problem anymore."

Chloe nodded. "That makes sense. But we couldn't even get to my back door. They'll stop us from getting into your yard."

"Do you know that for sure?"

"I don't know anything for sure."

"What if one of us climbs out on one of the branches?" said Elijah. "The longest one. And then they hang from it and swing back and forth, getting higher and higher, like they're on a swing in a playground or doing a gymnastics routine in the Olympics, and then, at the exact right moment, they let go and launch into my yard. Would that work?"

"Are you volunteering?" asked Chloe.

"It could be any one of us. I wouldn't do it if somebody else wanted to."

"There is absolutely no way somebody could make it all the way into your yard," said Chloe. "Not even close. And they'd have two broken legs."

"Okay, that's a problem."

"Yeah."

"Are we sure they'd break their legs?" Elijah asked.

"Why don't you try it and report back?"

"Nah."

"We're not that desperate yet," said Avery. "If we hit the point where we *need* to try your plan, we'll do it, but I think a few bones will break."

"But what if the branch sags down as they hang on the end of it? Maybe it bends enough that they can let go and land on the grass without getting hurt, then run into my yard."

"If the branch bent down, then you'd be next to the tree trunk, and it wouldn't have done you any good," said Chloe.

"That's true," said Elijah thoughtfully. "This is why I didn't volunteer to make the plan." He sighed. "Do you have anything to eat up here?"

"We're not going to starve," said Chloe.

"I never said anything about starving. I was just asking if you had a bag of chips or some pistachios or something."

"No."

"That's too bad. Pistachios would help take my mind off the situation."

The tree wobbled a bit.

Everybody froze.

Madison looked around, her eyes big. "Did everybody else feel that?"

Chloe nodded.

"I'm glad I'm not losing my mind," said Madison. "Not so glad they're tearing down the tree."

The tree wobbled again.

Chloe looked over the edge. The dirt was churned all around the bottom of the trunk. At least six tentacles were wrapped around it. She looked back at the others.

"Tell us the good news first," said Elijah.

"I never said I had any good news."

"Oh. I figured you were going to say, 'I have good news, and I have bad news.'"

"The good news is that the tree hasn't fallen over. The bad news is that it's definitely going to."

"That's pretty bad news," said Elijah.

"Yeah."

"Okay, so who's willing to break their legs?"

"Nobody is going to break their legs," said Avery. "We have to be smart. One of us has to climb down and make a run for it."

"Why are you looking at me when you say that?" asked Elijah.

"I'm not volunteering you," said Avery. "I'm volunteering myself."

"Seriously?" asked Chloe.

"I'm the fastest."

"Look, I don't want to die with everybody thinking I'm a total chicken, so I'll come with you," said Elijah.

"No," said Avery. "Only one of us is going. If two go, somebody will be slower. That person will get grabbed by a tentacle, and then the faster person will have to save them, and that defeats the purpose."

"But what if *you* get grabbed by a tentacle?" Madison asked.

"I won't."

"You've already been grabbed by one," Chloe pointed out.

"It won't happen again. They won't have the element of surprise."

"It's my yard," said Chloe. "I should go."

"Are you faster than me?"

"No."

"Then I'm going."

"I'm the slowest," said Madison. "So I definitely shouldn't go."

"We could distract them," said Elijah. "This tree house is falling apart anyway, so we could throw some pieces of wood in the opposite direction, and maybe they'll pop up there instead."

"That's actually a really good idea," said Avery.

"Thanks. I just thought of it and—"

"Don't overexplain," said Avery. "Accept the compliment."

"Thank you."

The tree wobbled again, much worse than the other times.

The wasp's nest fell off and dropped into Elijah's lap.

He let out a scream. "Get it off me! Get it off me!"

"Elijah—" said Chloe.

"Get it off me! I'm allergic! Get it off me! Don't let them sting me! I left my EpiPen in my bedroom! Get it off me! Get it off me!"

"Elijah—"

"If I die, I want it to be because of the monster with all the octopus arms, not wasps!"

"Elijah, calm down."

"*You* calm down! *You* calm down!"

"There are no wasps coming out of the nest."

Elijah looked at the nest more carefully. "That's true."

"Who knows how long ago they built that nest? It's empty. They're gone."

Elijah let out a sigh of relief. "I'd be lying if I said I'm not embarrassed, but at least I took our minds off our other problems for a little bit."

Chloe picked up the nest and was about to toss it over the edge of the tree house when she decided to use it to distract the tentacles when Avery made a run for it, so she placed it on the floor instead.

"Are you sure you want to do this?" she asked Avery.

The tree wobbled again.

"Yeah," said Avery.

"Okay," said Chloe. "We've got your back. What else can we do besides throw things to distract them?"

"You can sing really badly."

"Look! Look!" Madison frantically pointed to Chloe's house.

The back door was open.

Aunt Sandy peered out into the yard.

"Mom!" Madison shouted. "We need help! Call the police! Don't come outside!"

"Girls?" Aunt Sandy called out. "Girls?"

"Mom! Call the police!"

"I know you're still awake," said Aunt Sandy. "I can see the lights of your phones."

"Aunt Sandy!" Chloe shouted. "We're not in the tent! We're up in the tree house! Call the police!"

"Don't come outside!" Madison shouted. "Please don't come outside!"

"Madison, it's not nice to ignore your mother!" said Aunt Sandy. "Don't make me come out there in my bare feet!"

"What do we do?" asked Madison frantically. "How can we make her hear us?"

"She won't hear us until she comes outside," said Chloe. "So, the very second she does, we scream *very clearly* for her to go back inside and get help. We can't all scream at once. We need her to understand us. You're responsible for this. Got it?"

Madison nodded. "Yes, I've got it."

Aunt Sandy closed the door.

"No!" shouted Avery.

Chloe wanted to scream in frustration. Why hadn't her aunt bothered to come outside?

The tree gave another wobble. Chloe had no idea how many wobbles it was going to take for the tree to come crashing to the ground, but she didn't think it would be *that* many more.

Madison began to cry.

"Don't lose hope," said Avery. "I'm going to climb down what's left of the ladder and run to Elijah's yard. Nice and simple. Everybody is still on board with that plan, right?"

"I can't believe Mom didn't come outside," said Madison.

"We need to focus on things we can control," said Avery. "I'm disappointed too, but there's nothing we can do about it."

"She could have saved us."

"Madison, stop it. We can save ourselves. But for us to do that, we have to focus and work together, or we won't get out of this. Do you understand?"

"But she..." Madison wiped her eyes. "You're right. You're totally right."

The back door opened again.

Aunt Sandy stepped outside. She was wearing shoes.

CHAPTER 10

When Aunt Sandy had first opened the door, she'd looked annoyed.

When she stepped outside, her mouth dropped open in shock.

"Mom!" Madison shouted. "Go back inside and call the police!"

"Madison? What's happening?"

"Call the police!"

Aunt Sandy took a step toward the tree house.

Chloe wanted to scream at her aunt, but Avery was absolutely right. If they all screamed at once, Aunt Sandy wouldn't be able to understand them. Not that she was paying attention to what Madison was saying anyway.

"Mom! Listen to me! *Go! Back! Inside!*"

Aunt Sandy looked completely bewildered, but she did indeed take a step back.

A tentacle burst up from the ground next to her.

Then another. And another. And another.

Aunt Sandy shrieked.

Tentacles wrapped around her arms, legs, and waist.

"*Mom!*" cried Madison.

The tree wobbled again, but Chloe didn't care. She was too transfixed and horrified by what was happening to her aunt.

Aunt Sandy stooped down a bit, and suddenly Chloe could only see half her right leg.

The tentacles were pulling her under the ground!

"*Let me go! Let me go!*" Aunt Sandy screamed and struggled. It wasn't doing any good. Half her left leg also disappeared beneath the lawn.

"I'm coming, Mom!" Madison shouted. She scooted over to the ladder—what was left of it—and put her foot on the first rung.

"Don't!" Chloe told her. There was no way Madison could make it to Aunt Sandy in time to help. She'd simply meet the same fate.

But it wasn't as if Chloe could hold Madison back. This was her mother! If Chloe grabbed her cousin's arm and stopped her from going down the ladder, Madison would blame her for whatever happened for the rest of her life. Granted, that might not be very much longer, but still...

It was as if the lawn had become quicksand. Aunt Sandy had sunk to her waist.

"Help me, girls!" she screamed.

"What can we do?" Elijah asked, his voice frantic.

Chloe didn't answer. What *could* they do, besides go down there and get dragged underground by tentacles themselves?

She couldn't see which rung Madison was on, but she'd stopped descending the ladder.

"I love you, Madison!" Aunt Sandy shouted, as the tentacles pulled her so only her neck and head were visible.

"I'm coming!" Madison screamed.

Is Madison going to jump the rest of the way? Chloe wondered. It wasn't *that* far, and Madison *might* be okay. But she was already limping from before. She'd be doomed.

With a last shriek, Aunt Sandy disappeared beneath the ground.

Madison sobbed.

"Madison, get back here!" said Chloe.

Her cousin was crying too hard to answer.

"Come back up!" Chloe repeated. "They can reach you from there!"

Madison still didn't answer. Chloe couldn't blame her. But she needed to move to a safer place.

"Help me," Chloe told Avery. Both girls leaned over the side of the tree house and reached for Madison's arms. They wouldn't be able to hoist her if Madison refused to move, but they could at least encourage her to climb out of reach of the tentacles.

Madison climbed up. "They got her," she whimpered.

"We're going to figure this out, I promise," Chloe told her. It seemed like a promise that would be difficult to uphold, considering what had just happened to Aunt Sandy, but they all needed to stay calm.

"My mom is dead!" Madison wailed.

"No," said Avery. "Your mom is alive. *I promise!*"

"Weren't you *watching*?"

Avery nodded. "I sure was. And I didn't see her die. I saw her get pulled under the ground. Those are two completely different things."

"But she won't be able to breathe!"

"Madison, how much weird stuff has happened tonight? A lot, right?"

"Yes, a lot."

"So, based on all the weird stuff that's going on, like our phones all dying at the same time and your mom seeing the tent the way it used to be, not the way it is now, don't you think it's possible that your mom got taken someplace else?"

Avery had a point. This night had been so strange, why *couldn't* Aunt Sandy simply be hanging out in an underground cave or something? Maybe her worst problem right now was that she had dirt all over her new shoes.

Madison shrugged and sniffled.

"She's right," said Chloe. "I think your mom is fine. I mean, I'm sure she's scared, but there's no way those things killed her."

"She might be okay," said Madison, very quietly.

"She definitely is," said Avery. "We'll get her back. But to do that, we have to get out of our own mess."

The tree swayed. This time it wasn't just a wobble. It leaned at least three or four feet to the side before straightening again. Aunt Sandy had managed to distract the tentacles, but it was time to return their attention to that very important problem.

"I'm going that way," said Avery, pointing to Elijah's yard. "I need you to throw as much stuff as you can to keep the tentacles occupied. I'm good at gymnastics, so I'll somersault my way over them if I have to."

"When did you become good at gymnastics?" Chloe asked.

"Just now. In my imagination."

Chloe smiled. "Be careful."

"I'm always careful."

"No, you aren't. It's why we're best friends."

"I know you're trying to make this a special moment," said Elijah, "but you should hug so she can go."

Chloe gave Avery a hug. She didn't want to let go, but she forced herself to. Everything would be fine. Avery would make it to safety. She had to.

She quickly went down the ladder, despite the broken rungs.

Chloe, Madison, and Elijah began to throw things: Cans. Dolls. Pieces of broken wood. The wasp nest.

It was working! Not everything that landed had a tentacle pop up next to it, but the distraction seemed to be keeping them away from Avery!

That is, until one popped up right in front of her

She weaved around it.

Another one popped up.

She weaved around that one too.

One smacked her in the face.

Avery cried out and clutched her cheeks with both hands. She stumbled to the side, looking as if she might lose her balance.

"Don't fall!" Chloe shouted, as they continued to fling stuff from the tree house.

Avery managed to stay upright. She was almost to Elijah's yard!

The tentacle that had slapped her wrapped around her waist and began to drag her away from Elijah's property line.

No! She'd almost made it! It wasn't fair!

Avery had told everybody to stay up in the tree house so she wouldn't have to save them. Yet somebody needed to save her!

She struggled to move forward, but her bare feet slid in the grass.

Elijah should have given her his shoes. Though then she would've been running in shoes that were too big for her, and that would've caused its own problems.

They were running out of things to throw.

Avery slipped and she fell, landing on her stomach.

The tentacle continued to drag her.

The chair! They hadn't thrown the chair yet!

Chloe picked it up and hoisted it over her head. She didn't have time to aim, yet her aim had to be perfect. She had to help her best friend!

She flung the chair at the tentacle. *Please let it hit. Please let it hit.*

It almost hit. But not quite.

Chloe wanted to scream.

But Avery reached out and grabbed the chair. She twisted around and then bashed the chair into the tentacle, again and again. One of the legs broke off. Then the other. She continued hitting it...until the tentacle finally released its grip.

Avery got back up and ran again.

"Go!" Chloe shouted. "Run! Run!"

Another tentacle popped up. Avery, who was still holding the chair, took a swing and smacked it out of the way. Then she did the same with the next tentacle. And the next one. Large pieces of the chair kept flying off, but she was steps away from Elijah's yard.

When she struck the next tentacle, the seat flew out of her hands.

Two more steps. Only two more steps! Chloe cheered.

A tentacle sprouted from the ground in front of her, but

she leaped over it like she was training for hurdles in the summer Olympics.

Avery fell, landing hard with a loud "*ooomph!*"

But she'd fallen into Elijah's yard!

"She made it!" Chloe shouted. "She actually made it!" Would the tentacles follow her into Elijah's yard? Would she be able to get help?

Avery stood up. Brushed some dirt off her pajamas. She looked around the yard, as if very confused.

"Avery! Run for his house! Get inside!"

She didn't run. She walked slowly, as if trying to figure out where she was. She turned back toward the tree house, scratching her head and frowning.

"It's like she lost her memory. She has no idea what's going on," said Madison.

What if she walked back into Chloe's yard? What would happen?

Chloe wanted to shout to get her attention, but why bother? It wouldn't help. They just watched.

A light turned on in Elijah's back yard. His back door opened, and a woman wearing a fuzzy bathrobe stepped outside.

"Mom!" Elijah shouted. "Mom! I'm up here!"

She didn't look at him. Instead, she walked over to Avery. "Are you okay, Avery?"

"Mrs. Duncan?"

"I was making some tea and saw you in the yard. Are you all right? Why aren't you at home?"

"I—I don't know how I got here."

"Do you think you were sleepwalking?"

"Maybe."

"Have you done that before?"

"Not as far as I know."

Mrs. Duncan took Avery by the hand. "You were spending the night at Chloe's, right?"

Avery nodded. "We're camping in her backyard."

"Well, I'll walk you over to her mom, just to make sure everything's okay."

"Thank you."

Mrs. Duncan led Avery through the side yard between their two houses.

"Are we...saved?" Madison asked.

"Not if she doesn't remember any of it," said Chloe. "I think I just lost my best friend—and we lost our best runner."

CHAPTER 11

"What's our plan now?" Elijah asked.

"I don't know," Chloe admitted. "Your mom is going to take Avery to see my mom. They'll think it's really strange that she was in your backyard without any reason, so then my mom will come out to check on us."

"Why hasn't she come out yet?"

"Aunt Sandy likes to talk." She patted Madison on the shoulder. "No offense."

"It's okay," said Madison. Honestly, after her initial sobbing fit, Madison seemed to be handling the disappearance of her mother better than Chloe would in her position.

"So we're going back to the plan we tried with your aunt?" Elijah asked. "When your mom steps outside, you shout for her to call the police before the tentacles get her?"

"Yeah," said Chloe. "We just need my mom to *listen*. She'll know something's off because of what happened with Avery, so I think she'll get the message."

"That'll work," said Elijah. "There's no reason it won't, right?"

There were many reasons the plan might not work, including all that had happened to Aunt Sandy, but Chloe saw no benefit to listing them right now. "No reason at all," she said.

"We just have to hope she comes outside before the tree falls down," said Madison.

"Right," said Chloe.

How long would it take? Not very long, right? Elijah's mom would ring the front doorbell. Mom would answer. Elijah's mom would explain that she'd found Avery in her backyard, as if she'd been sleepwalking. Mom would thank her and take Avery inside. She'd get her a glass of water, sit her down on the couch, offer to call Avery's mom to come and get her, and then go out and check on Chloe and Madison. How long would that be? A couple of minutes?

A couple of minutes at the *most*.

"Do you think the tree will last that long?" asked Madison.

"Absolutely," said Chloe.

Chloe didn't know if the tentacles could hear them. It didn't seem that the tentacles themselves had ears, but maybe whatever creature lurked underneath the ground was listening in on their conversations. And surely, if it wanted to kill them, or drag them down into its lair, it would just do it, without concern for dramatic timing.

That said, Madison asked if the tree would last that long, and Chloe said "absolutely," and *that* was exactly when the tree began to truly sway back and forth.

With each movement, the tree swayed further. The tentacles were no longer messing around. They were going to take down this tree, and it was going to happen *soon*.

"What do we do?" Elijah asked, terrified.

"Hold on!" said Chloe.

It felt like being on a carnival ride, except there wasn't much to hold on to. And the tree house's existence meant when that thing crashed to the ground, it was going to send jagged pieces of wood flying everywhere, along with quite a few nails.

"I changed my mind!" said Chloe. "Don't hold on! Climb down!"

It was a good idea, but it would've been a much better idea if she'd come up with it sooner.

There was a thunderous cracking sound, which Chloe was pretty sure was the tree breaking free of its roots.

Chloe, Madison, and Elijah all screamed.

Chloe had heard that in moments like these, everything seemed to move in slow motion. She didn't know if it was your brain trying to give you more time to make the right decisions or your brain making sure you didn't miss a terrifying instant. But the tree did seem to fall in slow motion.

She slid forward in slow motion.

Grabbed the side of the tree house in slow motion.

Felt the side of the tree house break away in slow motion.

The ground was coming toward them in slow motion. It was going to hurt when they landed.

She could barely hear Madison and Elijah screaming, as if they were miles away. Chloe wasn't sure if that was a trick of her brain or if the sound of her own screaming was drowning them out.

It didn't matter. The impact was loud.

The tree house practically exploded, sending chunks of wood flying everywhere.

Everything went completely dark. Did the floodlight on the back of the house go out?

Oh. So this is what it's like to be dead, Chloe thought.

Chloe was glad everything was dark. She didn't want to have to look at her own dead body. That would be creepy and gross. She'd rather stay in the darkness forever.

Would she start floating away from her body?

If so, when would that happen? She hoped it was soon. No reason to waste time.

It hurt to be dead.

Specifically, it hurt her arm to be dead.

Truthfully, her arm didn't hurt the way she'd expect a dead arm to hurt. This was more the way she'd expect an arm to feel if it had been injured from a fall.

Maybe she had misread the situation and was, in fact, not dead.

Chloe opened her eyes.

She wasn't dead.

Neither were Madison and Elijah, though they weren't giggling or dancing around.

"Is everybody okay?" she asked.

"Not really," said Elijah. "This has been an awful night."

"I mean, are you *physically* okay?"

Elijah sat up. He brushed some wood particles off his shirt. "I think so."

"Madison?"

She nodded. "Something hit me in the stomach when we landed. But it didn't poke through or anything. I'll be all right."

Chloe sighed with relief. Her arm was still attached and didn't look broken. They'd all survived.

Of course, they still had the tentacles to contend with, and they no longer had their hiding spot.

She sat up straight and smacked her arm into some debris, which made her wince. Yes, she needed to pay a little more attention to her surroundings and not keep hurting herself.

She looked around. The tree had completely fallen over. The upper part had come close to hitting the corner of Chloe's house but hadn't struck it. The tree house had been demolished. Parts of it were scattered everywhere. Some branches had broken off the tree in the fall, but most of them remained attached, creating a big woodsy, leafy canopy over much of the yard.

Maybe the tree falling over hadn't been such a bad thing.

They were obviously much closer to the ground now, and the ground was a dangerous place to be. But as long as she, Madison, and Elijah stayed on the trunk of the tree, the tentacles would have to squirm up through the branches to get to them.

They weren't "safe" as in, *Ahhhh, this is delightful. Let's all relax and get some much-needed sleep.* They weren't even "safe" as in, *Let's allow ourselves to relax for two consecutive seconds.* But they might be "safe" as in, *As long as we pay really close attention and don't lose focus for a split second, maybe the tentacles won't grab us before Mom comes out to see what's going on.*

Better than nothing.

"Want to know the worst part?" asked Elijah.

"What?" asked Chloe.

"We now know for sure that nobody can hear us. Because if a whole tree can crash down in your backyard and nobody notices or comes to see what happened, what is going to get their attention?"

"I'd given up noise drawing them outside before the tree crashed," said Chloe.

"Oh," said Elijah. "I hadn't. It's probably because you've been out here longer than me."

Madison frowned. "I wonder if I'm an orphan?"

Elijah frowned too. "Yeah, you're right. I'm sorry. That's not what I meant. I didn't mean that it was literally the worst part. I was trying to make conversation."

"I think it's okay if we all don't talk," said Madison.

"Yeah, yeah, I understand."

Chloe wondered if Madison's crush on Elijah had disappeared. She had more important things to think about than boys. Though, as much as he got on Chloe's nerves, she did hope that after they survived this mess, Elijah and Madison would live happily ever after.

Something to worry about later.

"If we want to talk about the best part," said Chloe, "at least the tentacles are leaving us alone."

Elijah looked around the yard. "You're right. That's kind of cool, at least."

"Yeah."

Elijah furrowed his brow in deep concentration, and then suddenly his face lit up with excitement. "Hear me out!"

Chloe and Madison each gave him a nod.

"What if the sound of the tree falling drove them away? Maybe the sound or the vibrations or whatever sent the tentacles underground. This could be our chance! Maybe we could run to my yard!"

"But, to think of it another way, they might *not* be hiding, and if we try to run to your yard, they'll get us," said Chloe.

Elijah picked up a piece of wood and threw it into a bare patch on the lawn.

Nothing happened.

"See?" he said. "I think I'm right."

"You might be!" said Madison.

"I'll go first," said Elijah. "If I make it to my yard and forget all about you, then both of you follow! There's no time to waste, so I'm going."

Elijah stood up and then hesitated.

"Actually," he said, "do you think I should make a run for it or try to walk really slowly and softly?"

"Run," said Madison.

Elijah nodded. Then he leaped off the tree and sprinted for his yard.

He's going to make it, Chloe thought. *He's really going to—*

Elijah screamed as a tentacle burst out of the ground and wrapped around his leg.

Several more popped out.

Chloe put her hand over her mouth as she gaped in horror.

The tentacles dragged him under the dirt, the same way they had Aunt Sandy, and he screamed all the way down.

CHAPTER 12

For a few seconds, all Chloe and Madison could do was stare at the Elijah-sized hole in the ground. Then it closed, the same way it had with Aunt Sandy, as if it had never been there. Even with all the tentacle action, that was freaky.

"Did that really happen?" Madison asked.

"Yeah," said Chloe, barely able to speak.

"Is it going to happen to us?"

"No," said Chloe. "We know that his theory was wrong. We're staying right where we are."

"What if I got him killed by telling him to run?" Madison's lip trembled.

"It was his idea. You didn't tell him he *had* to run. He asked your opinion. My guess is that the same thing would've happened if he tried to tiptoe quietly. So it's not your fault."

"Maybe—maybe he and my mom are figuring out a way to escape."

"I bet they are," said Chloe. "They totally are." She wasn't sure Madison felt more reassured.

"Should we, I don't know, see if we can dig down into the holes?"

"No. We should definitely not do that. That's a good way to get dragged into one of them ourselves."

"But what if they need our help?"

"Of course they need our help! But we're trapped here. There's nothing we can do."

"Are we being, like, cowardly?" Madison asked.

"No. We're being smart. If we let the tentacles get us, we'll all wind up underground, and we might never get out."

"They could be dead," said Madison.

"Stop it," said Chloe. "Don't talk like that. We have no idea what happened to them, and we're not doing ourselves any good focusing on that."

"But we can't hear them. Shouldn't we hear them screaming?"

"Maybe their mouths are full of dirt."

"But—"

"Madison, we're in uncharted territory here. I don't

understand where these tentacles came from, or what they want, or what they're doing. I'm—"

Suddenly there was the creak of a screen door swinging open. It was Mom, with Avery right behind her.

"Mom! Stay where you are!" Chloe shouted.

But Mom couldn't hear her yet. She stepped out into the backyard.

Aunt Sandy hadn't wanted to go outside. Mom did. She took a step forward before registering the shouting.

Avery's eyes widened as she stepped outside after her.

"Mrs. Whitting! Come back inside!"

Avery reached out and grabbed the back of Mom's shirt, just as a tentacle lunged out of the ground and wrapped around her leg.

"No!" Chloe and Madison screamed at the same time.

Chloe couldn't just stand there and wait to see what happened. Yes, the tentacles could get her too, but this was her *mother*. She leaped off the tree trunk.

Three more tentacles came out of the ground and wrapped around Mom.

Avery grabbed one of Mom's arms as the tentacles began to drag her into the ground, which now looked like an open pit.

Somehow, Chloe managed to dodge the tentacles and

reach Mom. She took Mom's other arm, and she and Avery pulled as hard as they could.

Mom looked terrified and confused.

"I won't let you go!" Chloe promised, as Mom's arm slipped out of Avery's hands.

As Chloe was desperately trying to save her mother, Madison yelled, "Guys, the door is open! The path is clear!"

"Go back inside!" Chloe told Avery. "Call the police!"

Avery nodded and ran back inside the house. Chloe focused her attention on her mother.

Four more tentacles emerged and wrapped around her.

Mom looked Chloe directly in the eyes. "Let me go! Save yourself!"

"No!" Chloe refused. She didn't care how strong the tentacles were. She was *not* letting go. Nothing could make her.

A tentacle slithered over her arm.

This one had thorns.

It tightened around her arm, digging into her skin.

Chloe winced in pain but didn't budge.

The tentacle tightened even more.

Chloe couldn't hold on. With a last "I love you!" Mom was pulled into the pit with a shriek.

Had she lost *both* her parents?

She could see Avery through the doorway. She looked still and bewildered.

Avery didn't remember what was happening in the backyard...again!

She pushed open the door.

No! Chloe wished they'd created a secret best friend code word for a situation like this.

The tentacle around Chloe's arm yanked her, hard. She stumbled toward the edge of the pit.

Avery stepped outside.

Again it was like a light switch flipped on. The realization of all that had happened—was happening—struck Avery at once. Chloe could see it on her face.

Avery lunged forward and grabbed Chloe's arm.

Chloe hadn't been able to hold on to her own mother, so how could Avery help her? She was doomed.

No. Don't think like that. You only have one tentacle holding you. Mom had a bunch of them. Look for an opportunity.

Chloe didn't have a weapon. All she had were her teeth. She needed something sharp.

Like...thorns.

"Twist it around and make it stab itself!" Chloe said.

"I don't understand!"

"It has thorns! Slam the other part of the tentacle into its own thorns!"

"Like this," Madison said with an angry growl.

Madison?

Chloe wanted to scold her cousin for putting herself in more danger, but for now, she was relieved to have the help.

Madison grabbed part of the tentacle and smashed it onto the segment wrapped around Chloe's arm. Chloe tried to move her arm back and forth, sawing the creature with its own thorn.

The tentacle unfurled itself from Chloe's arm and let out a shriek.

The previous shrieks had been agony to hear, but the girls had gotten used to them. But the sound that came from the pit was overwhelmingly loud. Chloe, Avery, and Madison all put their hands over their ears, and Madison dropped to her knees.

When it stopped, Chloe's ears were ringing.

All three of them were together. They could—

Nope. Some tentacles had sprouted to block the back door.

Seriously? thought Chloe. This was long past being ridiculous.

They ran back to the "safety" of the tree. Behind them, the pit closed with a rumble.

For a few moments, they just tried to catch their breath.

"I'm so sorry about your mom," Avery told Chloe.

Chloe shook her head. "My mom is okay. Aunt Sandy is okay. Elijah is okay. If any of us get dragged down there, we'll be okay too. Nobody is dead in this yard, all right?"

Madison nodded.

"All right," said Avery.

"What do you remember?"

Avery sighed. "As soon as I stepped into Elijah's yard, it was like I woke up from a dream. I figured I must have sleep-walked out of the tent. Sleptwalk? What's the right word?"

"It doesn't matter," said Chloe.

"Mrs. Duncan walked me to your house, and your mom was really concerned about me, so we went outside to see if you and Madison knew what had happened. As soon as we left the house, *bam*, I remembered everything again. When I went back inside, that part of my memory was gone. I was standing in your kitchen with absolutely no clue how I'd gotten there. I remembered going outside with your mom, but that was it. I could see the tent, and everything in the backyard looked fine through the window. It was like Elijah

133

said—the yard looked the way it was before we crawled into our sleeping bags."

"So there's no way to send one of us for help," said Madison.

"I don't think so," said Avery.

"Well, that's a bummer."

"I think our earlier plans had merit," said Chloe. "But they didn't work. Not even a little. So we have to figure out something else."

"I hope you have a good idea," said Avery. "Because I've got nothing."

"I would love to tell you that I have an amazing idea," said Chloe. "But I also don't want to lie to you. So...no. I've got nothing. Madison?"

Madison sighed. "Nope."

"Great," said Chloe.

"This is not going well,'" said Avery.

Chloe paused. "I mean, when we started, the promise that the sun would rise and make everything all better sounded good. But now we know we'd be in just as much trouble as we are now, except we'd be thirstier and have the sun in our eyes."

"True," said Madison. "But people would notice that we're gone. Mrs. Duncan would come looking for Elijah."

"And then she'd get pulled under the lawn like everybody else."

"Right. So then we'd have three adults missing. And my mom has to go to work tomorrow." Madison thought about that. "No, I guess it's Saturday. She has work on Monday. At *some* point she has work, and so does your mom, and so does Mrs. Duncan. Somebody would say, 'Hey, why aren't they at work?' and when they ignored all their phone calls, somebody would eventually call the police and have them come over to check it out."

"Would they look in the backyard?" asked Chloe.

"The cops wouldn't investigate a missing person report and not bother to look in their backyard. And for all we know, this is happening in the front yard too."

"No," said Avery. "I walked through the front yard, and it was fine."

"Oh, okay. Still, the cops would knock on the door, and when nobody answered, they'd walk around the house to investigate."

"And then the cops would get dragged underground," Chloe pointed out.

"Maybe," said Madison. "But then they'd send more officers to look for those officers, and more officers to look for *those* officers, and eventually someone would figure out that something really bizarre was happening around here, and they'd come prepared."

"Or the tentacles and pit would swallow an infinite number of cops."

Madison pursed her lips, and Chloe tried to be more optimistic.

"If we sit here, eventually somebody might figure out what's going on and save us. But it could take a few days. I'm not sure we have a few hours. I'm not sure we have a few *minutes*. It's not like if we ask the tentacles to go away, they will."

"Are you sure about that?" asked Madison. "Have we even tried being nice to them? Maybe the problem is that we've been rude. Good manners are important."

Chloe stared at her for a moment. Madison sounded like she was practicing for a beauty pageant, not plotting for survival. "I hope you're joking."

Madison stuck her tongue out at her. "Of course I was joking."

"Okay, good."

"Did you really think I wasn't?"

"I didn't know!"

"Do you think that little of me?" asked Madison, hurt in her voice.

"I knew you were joking," Avery reassured her.

"Thank you."

"How was I supposed to know?" Chloe asked. "Your mom just got dragged down into a pit. That will mess up someone's sense of humor."

"You should be impressed that I was able to make any kind of joke!" said Madison.

"Now that I know you were kidding, yes, I'm very impressed," said Chloe. "Good job, Cousin."

"You're being sarcastic."

"And since my mom got dragged into the same pit as your mom, you should be impressed that I can be sarcastic."

"Fine. Great job being sarcastic." Madison rolled her eyes.

"Enough," said Avery. "I'm glad you're both coping well enough to bicker, but that doesn't get us anywhere."

"I'm still waiting for your idea," said Chloe.

"I've got one."

"What is it?"

"We fight back."

CHAPTER 13

"What do you mean?" asked Madison.

"You know what the word 'fight' means, right?" asked Avery.

"Your mom didn't get dragged into a pit, so you don't get any credit for being sarcastic," said Chloe.

"Fine," said Avery. "I apologize. What I'm saying is that we've been trying to outrun these things the whole time. It hasn't worked. It may never work. But we know we can hurt them to drive them away. So that's what we should do."

"With what?" asked Chloe.

"We gather the boards from the tree house that still have nails in them. And we pull the nails from the rotting wood and pound them into a board for each of us. Then we'll step off this tree, and we'll bash those tentacles until this back-yard is a lake of black ooze."

"That sounds disgusting," said Madison. She hadn't com-plained about the ooze on her pajamas, though. Chloe was proud of her.

"Yes, but it's the good kind of disgusting." Avery smiled. "We can't wait this out. And for all we know, your moms and Elijah are fine for now, but every minute counts. So let's do this. Who's with me?"

"We don't have a hammer," said Chloe.

"I know. We can use another piece of wood or a rock. Who's with me?"

"I'm with you," said Madison.

"Me too," said Chloe.

The girls went to work. Finding three boards that suited their needs was fairly easy, and they even had nails already in them. The nails were rusty, although the tentacles proba-bly weren't worried about having to get a tetanus shot.

The more challenging part was gathering more nails. They were relatively easy to find, but even though much of the wood was in terrible shape, getting the nails out of them was really difficult. And then pounding them into the planks of wood, using other wood as a hammer, was also a real pain.

"This is going to take forever," said Chloe.

"You're right," said Avery. "We've each got a plank with three nails?"

"Mine only has two," said Madison.

"So we've each got a plank with two or three nails?"

"Yes."

"Let's work with what we've got. Is everybody ready?"

"Not really," said Chloe. "But it's not like we have a choice."

"You're absolutely right. Now, remember, we can't leave the yard."

"Why not?" asked Madison. "If we have the chance to escape, shouldn't we take it?"

"If you leave, you'll completely forget what happened to your mom, and you won't try to rescue her."

Madison nodded. "That's a very good reason."

Chloe sighed. "There's an axe in my garage that Dad used to cut wood. We've got all kinds of stuff there that would work better. It's all so close."

"And yet so far," said Avery.

"I wish there were a way to..." Chloe's eyes widened. "My scrapbook! Where's my scrapbook?"

"I haven't seen it since the tree fell. Why?"

"We have to find it. Help me look!"

It took a couple of minutes, but Madison found it wedged in with some branches. She handed it to Chloe, who removed the pencil that was tucked inside and began to write.

> Chloe, call 911. Tell them to come right away. Mom fell into a sinkhole in the backyard. Get the axe and baseball bat out of the garage, then go into the backyard to help. Do not, under any circumstances, go into the backyard until you've made the call and you have these things.

She tore that page out of the journal, then wrote the same note for Madison. Then she wrote a similar note to Avery, changing it to "Chloe's mom."

She folded Madison's paper in half several times, until it was a tiny square, then handed it to her. "Put it in your mouth."

"Why would I do that?"

"You'd have no reason to check your pocket. If you're carrying it while you're swinging around a big plank, you might drop it. But if you find yourself in Elijah's yard with no memory of how you got there, and there's a piece of paper in your mouth, you're going to see what's on it."

"That's a really good idea," said Madison. "What if I swallow it? I'm getting hungry."

"Don't swallow it. It's the best of both plans," said Chloe.

"We jump off this tree, and we try to mess these tentacles up as much as we can. However, if we have the opportunity to escape into my house or out of the backyard, we take it."

"I like that," said Avery. She took her note from Chloe, folded it up into a square, and popped it into her mouth. "Mmmm. Yummy. Nutritious."

Chloe folded up her own note and put it in her mouth. "Let's do this. Who knows? It might even be fun," she said, though she sounded like she did when the dentist tried to ask her questions while cleaning her teeth.

Avery laughed. "If it's fun, there's really something wrong with us."

"Well, we knew that already." Chloe took a practice swing with her plank. "I'm ready if you both are."

"I'm ready," said Madison.

"Ready," said Avery.

They jumped off the fallen tree.

/////

"What's wrong?" Chloe asked. She'd been told to be home from Avery's by 6:30, and it was 6:29. Dinner of meat loaf, mashed potatoes, and broccoli was on the table.

"Nothing," said Mom.

Chloe frowned. "You don't look like it's nothing."

"Your dad didn't come home from work, and he's not answering his phone. His battery must have died. Did I forget he was stopping somewhere on his way home?"

"He's not *that* late." Dad usually got home a few minutes after 6:00. Half an hour was nothing. Heavy traffic could explain this.

"I know. I'm just surprised he didn't answer my texts or my calls."

"Should you call his boss or someone he works with?"

"No, no, no," said Mom. "He's not even half an hour late. I've just had this feeling that... No, I'm sorry, honey. I shouldn't be saying things like that. Your father will be home any minute now, so go get washed up for dinner."

As Chloe washed her hands, she couldn't help feeling a little queasy.

From a completely logical perspective, she knew that the overwhelming likelihood was that Dad was perfectly fine, and his car would pull into the driveway any minute, and they'd all sit down to enjoy Mom's mediocre meat loaf and lumpy mashed potatoes.

But she agreed with Mom. Something felt wrong.

Of course, her dear mother was the one who'd put that into her head. Mom tended to overreact to things.

Chloe sat next to Mom on the couch, and they watched some mindless TV for a while.

Dinner got cold. Finally, they threw it away. Neither of them had an appetite.

/////

Dad did not come home that night. The police said they would follow up on any leads, but they had absolutely nothing to go on yet. Mom explained that he would never just *not* come home unless something was terribly wrong. She got ahold of one of his coworkers, who said that, yes, he'd left their office building as usual.

Mom sat on the edge of Chloe's bed and assured her that everything was going to be all right. Dad wouldn't just leave them.

"I wasn't worried about that," said Chloe. "I'm worried that something *happened* to him."

Mom began to cry. "I'm worried about *everything*," she admitted.

/////

Dad did not report to work the next day, and he did not come home that evening. He was officially a "missing person." Posters went up all around town, and the police did everything they could to find him.

Nobody had seen him. Nobody had seen his car.

This went on for a week.

"Look," said one of the officers, talking to Mom. "We know it happens. Sometimes a husband and father, even if he seems happy, might have reasons to get in his car and drive away from everything."

"Don't you dare say that!" Mom looked so angry that Chloe worried she might slap the cop. Chloe really didn't want her mother to get arrested for assaulting a police officer. "Don't you dare say that in front of my daughter!"

"I apologize, ma'am," said the officer. "What I'm saying is that we have to look at all possibilities here."

"I know that. But he wouldn't just..." Mom cried, as she had pretty much had all week.

Chloe gave her a hug. She wasn't sure it made either of them feel any better.

/////

"Do you think he'll ever come back?" asked Avery. The two of them hadn't talked about Chloe's dad much after the first couple of days. Chloe appreciated that Avery reminded her of her old life, her normal life, and they mostly talked about school, music, and movies. Anything but her missing father.

"Yes," said Chloe.

But she was lying to her best friend. It had been a month. There was absolutely no sign of him. No sightings from anywhere in the country. Chloe had overheard Mom and Aunt Sandy discussing it, and Aunt Sandy had joked that maybe Dad bleached his hair and mustache blond and was sitting on a beach somewhere and getting a tan. Like Madison, Aunt Sandy wasn't the best judge of when a particular joke would go over well with the listener.

Dad wasn't coming back.

Maybe he'd left them. Maybe he was dead. Either way, it was childish for Chloe to believe she'd see him again.

It was heartbreaking.

She was sad all the time.

But then the sadness shifted into a different emotion.

Anger.

She didn't know who she should be mad at. If Dad had left them, then he was the obvious target of her rage, but she didn't want to direct all her anger his way, just in case none of this was his fault. Like if he'd been kidnapped. So who was left? She couldn't be mad at Mom. Yes, she directed some of her anger Mom's way, but it wasn't on purpose.

Chloe was filled with anger, all the time, and nothing made it go away. She listened to happy music. She listened to angry music. She tried to blow off steam playing softball, but when she threw the ball a little *too* hard at one of her fellow players, Coach lectured her, and she quit the team.

She punched her pillow a lot.

She made really angry movies in her mind. She wrote angry poetry.

Camping in the backyard with Avery was supposed to be fun, like before Dad had vanished without a trace.

She'd tried to control her anger, and she'd gotten a lot better at it, but it was still there, under the surface, all the time.

As Chloe jumped off the tree, holding her plank with the nails in it, she knew she could use her anger as a weapon. In this instance, that was okay—good even.

Because she was going to take out all her feelings from the past year on these tentacles.

CHAPTER 14

Chloe was energized!

Okay, "energized" was too strong of a word. Given the choice, she'd rather be inside, sipping hot chocolate and watching a movie. But since she didn't have a choice...she was ready.

Was she scared? Yeah. Was she absolutely *terrified*? Also yeah. But there'd been plenty of times in the past few months when she'd have loved the opportunity to smash something to bits, and if these tentacles were going to be on the receiving end of her fury, it was their own fault. Nobody had invited them here.

Avery, Chloe, and Madison stepped away from the tree, waiting for their enemy to strike.

Nothing happened.

Where were they?

Maybe the tentacles knew they were in serious trouble and had retreated underground.

That seemed kind of ridiculous, yet they weren't popping up. They *always* popped up. What was their deal?

The girls each took another step. Avery and Madison looked confused.

Were the tentacles messing with them?

Or maybe, having claimed three victims, the creature beneath the ground was sated for the time being. Maybe Chloe, Avery, and Madison could casually stroll into her house without anything trying to cause them harm.

Chloe took another tentative step forward.

A tentacle burst out of the ground in front of her.

Now things were back on track.

Chloe smacked the tentacle with the plank. She didn't get it with one of the nails, but it was a really hard hit, and the tentacle dropped and flopped around as if she'd broken it.

It wasn't good sportsmanship to hit an opponent after they'd fallen. But the situation didn't call for a good sport. She bashed the tentacle, again and again, hoping to turn it into a pool of tentacle goo. It retracted into the ground, and if it was smart, it would stay down there.

She looked over. A tentacle had emerged next to Avery. She struck it with her own plank, and she *did* get it with a nail. The screech was wonderfully, gloriously loud. Better than Chloe's favorite song. She didn't even cover her ears.

Avery gave the plank a twist. The tentacle pulled away, spraying black ooze, and then tried to slide back underground. But Avery hit it again, getting it with a different nail. She was really good at this.

Madison took a swing and missed.

Chloe heard a tentacle spring up behind her.

Trying to trick me, huh?

She spun around, swinging the plank, and smacked it so hard that she was surprised the tentacle didn't tear in half.

"Is that the best you can do?" she shouted, accidentally spitting out the note in her mouth as she said it.

Another tentacle wrapped around her leg. Okay, she was getting overconfident, thanks to rage and adrenaline, and she needed to take this a little more seriously.

She jabbed the tentacle with a rusty nail, trying to make sure she hit it hard enough to do some damage but not hard enough that the nail got her in the leg. As the beast shrieked, it slithered away from her leg, leaving an oily black stain.

With a cry of fury, she smashed the plank into another

tentacle. This was...well, she couldn't call it "*fun*," but it was satisfying.

Avery let out a battle cry of her own. Her plank broke in half with her hit.

Okay, that was a problem. Though they'd gotten off to a strong start, they were wildly outnumbered.

Avery dropped the piece of her plank.

Madison swung at a tentacle. This time she didn't miss.

"Come on!" Chloe shouted. "This is pathetic! You can do better than that!"

"I'm doing the best I can!" Madison insisted.

"No, no, I wasn't talking to you. I was talking to the tentacles."

"Why are you offering them encouragement?"

"I'm not! I'm trying to make them mad!"

"Why are you trying to make them mad?"

"It's what you're supposed to say in a fight! Everybody knows that! It's in the movies!"

Avery shook her head. "I think you two are getting distracted!"

She was correct.

Madison hit another one, and the plank flew out of her hands. She glanced at Chloe's house. The door was still open.

She ran for it.

Madison ran like a football player in a game where both teams were tied and only a few seconds were left on the clock. Like she was only a few yards from scoring a touchdown and nothing in the world was going to stop her from winning the game.

Or she ran like a twelve-year-old girl who knew she could save her life and the lives of her friends and family by making it inside the house.

A tentacle started to spring up, and she jumped over it—a jump so high that Chloe wouldn't have believed it if she hadn't witnessed it herself.

Madison swerved around another tentacle.

And then she dove—actually dove—through the doorway.

Chloe wanted to stare in shock and amazement, and think about which sports teams Madison might join with her hidden athletic talent, but Chloe was not remotely safe, and there were plenty of tentacles left to fight. She couldn't relax yet. Her and Avery's lives were still very much in danger.

Avery ran for the plank Madison had dropped and scooped it up. She immediately spun around and bashed a tentacle with it.

Chloe smacked another tentacle.

Avery let out a battle cry again and hit another one.

Chloe followed her lead. These battle cries felt good. They should've been doing that from the beginning.

Meanwhile, the tentacles appeared to have learned from their mistake. Several of them had stretched across the back door, blocking the way in and out.

A tentacle tried to wrap itself around her waist, but a well-placed hit made it rethink that strategy.

One wrapped around her ankle. She made it go away.

Then one wrapped around her other ankle. She struck this one too hard, hurting her foot, and it still didn't let go. It yanked her off her feet, and the plank popped out of her hands. As she landed on her back, she watched the board fall toward her in slow motion.

It hit her in the stomach...nail-side up. It hurt, but it could have been *so* much worse.

She sat up, just as a tentacle wrapped around her arm.

A different tentacle shoved Avery forward. Actually shoved her! Like it was a great big arm. She stumbled forward, tripped over some branches from the tree, and then fell over.

Chloe grabbed her plank and jabbed the nail deep into

the tentacle that held her arm. It loosened its grip, and she pulled her arm away from it.

Avery got back up.

It would sure be nice if Madison came outside with help.

How long would it take somebody to spit out a piece of paper, read what was written on it, decide if they believed the message or not, call the police, retrieve the weapons from the garage, and return to the backyard?

The answer: too long.

Chloe got back up. Her arms were getting tired. She hadn't trained for this.

Avery swung and missed. Her friend, too, looked like exhaustion was setting in.

Maybe they could run for Elijah's yard.

Chloe moved in that direction. Three tentacles popped up, dissuading her of that idea.

It had been naive to think they could defeat this creature with the remnants of a destroyed tree house. They were up against a being that defied all comprehension. Old lumber wasn't going to stop it.

She wanted to cry. But she was *not* going to cry. She was not going to let this thing believe it had the upper hand.

She was, however, going to retreat to the tree.

Chloe ran and jumped on the trunk. Avery either had the same idea or followed Chloe's lead. They stood on the trunk, holding their planks at the ready, trying to catch their breath.

A few moments later, Avery said, "We didn't do so bad."

"Nope."

"Could've done better."

"Yep."

"But Madison made it inside. That's really good. I mean, maybe she'll come out here with some dynamite."

"We don't own any dynamite."

"You sure? Maybe your mom keeps some just in case?"

"Pretty sure."

A tentacle lunged at Chloe's leg. She smashed her plank into it a few times, and it retreated.

"This isn't safe anymore," she said.

"It was never safe," said Avery. "But it's safer than the lawn. They can only pop up next to the tree, not through it."

"You have a point. I wish we could sit down."

"I wouldn't."

"I didn't say I was considering it. I said I wished we could."

"I wish we could too. A recliner would also be nice. Or a hammock."

"Oh, yeah," said Chloe. "I could go for a hammock and a bowl of fruit."

"What kind of fruit?"

"Watermelon. And maybe some grapes."

"I'd have pineapple," said Avery.

"Pineapple has those stringy parts that get stuck in my teeth."

"That's true, but we could use the rusty nails as toothpicks."

The girls laughed. Well, it wasn't true laughter, but it was close enough.

Chloe's arms felt like they were on fire. She'd really been hitting those tentacles *hard*. "I guess we wait to see if anything happens with Madison."

Chloe hit another tentacle. This time the plank flew out of her hands, before landing several feet away. "That's disappointing," she said.

Avery nodded.

"I'm happy to wait. I mean, I'm not *happy* about it, but it's the idea that makes the most sense."

Two tentacles slithered up the tree trunk right next to Avery. She slammed the plank down on the first one as she took a step away from the second one.

The tentacles were no longer going to leave them alone while they were on the tree.

The tree shifted a bit.

"What was that?" asked Chloe.

The tree shifted again.

"I have a theory," said Avery, "but it's not going to make you happy."

"Then maybe keep it to yourself."

They stood there for a moment.

"Okay, tell me."

"I think they're digging under the tree to take the entire thing down there with them."

"You're right," said Chloe. "That theory doesn't make me happy at all."

CHAPTER 15

Were things better or worse than they had been before their decision to fight back?

On the "better" side, Madison had made it inside the house with a note in her mouth. Their situation *could* improve at some point.

On the "worse" side, they'd discovered that they could not, in fact, defeat the creature with the wreckage of Chloe's tree house. And also, if Avery's guess was correct, at some point in the near future, this entire tree was going to be pulled into its own sinkhole, taking them along with it.

"How long do you think it would take those tentacles to dig a hole big enough for the tree to fall through?" Chloe asked.

"Depends on how many tentacles are down there and

how deep they want the hole to be," Avery said. "Basically, I have no idea."

"You know what would be nice?"

"What?"

"If they dug the hole, and the tree fell into it, and it squished whatever monster is under there."

"You're right," said Avery. "That would be nice."

"Probably won't happen, though."

"Probably not." Avery paused to hit another tentacle with her plank. "But we can hope."

Chloe stomped on a tentacle. She hated the way it felt under her bare feet. Worse than stepping on a snake, not that she'd ever stepped on a snake. "Remind me to wear cleats the next time we go camping," she told Avery.

Chloe stomped on it a few more times, then shifted along the tree trunk until she was out of reach.

"You're my best friend," Chloe said. "I want you to know that."

"I already know we're best friends. 'You're my best friend' is something you say when you think we might be speaking our final words to each other."

"No," said Chloe. "It's something you can say when your best friend buys you a really cool T-shirt."

"I didn't buy you a T-shirt."

"Look, I'm not saying that we are going to die, but I am saying that it's not completely out of the question. You know, before we're really old and stuff. So I wanted to make sure I said it to you."

"I appreciate that," said Avery. "But don't say anything like that for the rest of the night. You can compliment me on how many tentacles I've destroyed, and I'll praise you for the same, but I don't want to hear any more talk about what great friends we are, because we've got a lot of friendship left to go, okay?"

"Okay. I just—"

"You've already explained yourself."

"I won't say anything else that sounds like the last thing we'll ever say to each other," Chloe promised. A tentacle slithered up onto the trunk next to her.

Avery went over and bashed the tentacle until it left. "One of the nails came out."

Somebody screamed.

Madison.

Her cousin was standing at the back door, with several tentacles squirming all over her. She wouldn't have seen the tentacles blocking the way until she stepped through the doorway, and she would never have expected something like that! Chloe should've included that information in the note.

Madison kept screaming as she flailed around.

Black ooze sprayed into the air, and a two-foot-long piece of a tentacle hit the ground.

Then another piece hit the ground.

Madison wasn't just flailing around in panic—she was flailing around with an axe!

She'd read the note! She'd gotten the woodcutting axe out of the garage!

Another piece of tentacle dropped to the ground. It was easier to see what Madison was doing now. She also had an aluminum baseball bat. She made a path for herself as she chopped through the tentacles. She stepped out into the yard and tossed the bat to Chloe.

Chloe caught it and grinned.

A couple of tentacles sprang up and tried to stop Madison, but some quick swings of the axe took care of them. She hurried over to the tree and jumped up there with the others.

"I think I ruined my pajamas," she said, gesturing to the black gunk on them.

"I'll buy you a new pair," said Chloe. "Thank you."

"Thank you for writing the note. Do you know how weird it is to suddenly find yourself inside with no memory of how you got there and a folded-up piece of paper in your mouth?"

"Really weird?"

"Yes, really weird."

Chloe swung the bat like she was trying to hit a home run. The tentacle she hit didn't go back under the lawn. It dropped onto the ground and twitched.

"Did you call the police?" Avery asked.

"I said there was an emergency."

"That's good. If you'd told them about the tentacles, they would've thought it was a joke."

"I didn't remember anything about the tentacles when I was in there. I honestly thought you two were playing a prank on me, but I called for my mom and your mom, and nobody was around, so I decided to trust the note."

"We're glad you did," said Chloe, bashing another tentacle. The bat worked much better than the plank. She felt like she could knock out a hundred of those things.

"Can I have a turn?" Avery asked, gesturing to the axe.

"Sure," said Madison, handing it over. Avery did a quick test swing, then chopped a tentacle in half. It thrashed around. Chloe was glad that the pieces didn't continue to move after they'd been chopped off. Nobody wanted to see that kind of thing.

"Actually, can I trade you?" Chloe asked.

"Yeah, no problem." Avery handed Chloe the axe, and Chloe gave her the baseball bat. The bat was awesome, but the axe was clearly the superior weapon, especially for what she planned to do.

"Don't freak out," said Chloe.

"What are you going to say that would make me freak out?" Avery asked.

"It's not what I'm going to say. It's what I'm going to do."

"Chloe..."

"I'm going to try to get my mom and Aunt Sandy out of the ground."

"What?" Avery asked. "How?"

"We didn't have an axe before. I can dig for them! Maybe they aren't too deep!"

"Chloe, no. We're not digging for your mom!"

"How do we know we can't chop through the ground, reach down there, and pull them out?"

"Because if you could just 'reach down there' and grab them, we'd hear them calling out to us!"

Avery had a good point, but Chloe wasn't in the mood to listen. They had an *axe*! And a baseball bat! They were basically invincible. Sure, the police were on their way, but they'd already established that it would probably take a few sets of police officers to make any real progress.

Chloe stepped off the tree.

"Don't do it," said Avery. "It's a terrible idea."

"I don't agree with that."

Why leave her mom in the pit when she might be able to save her? The terrible idea was *not* doing anything to get her out of there.

"Chloe, please."

"You're the one who said we should fight!"

"But not on their home turf!"

"You didn't just lose your mom."

"That's not fair."

"I'm going," said Chloe. She stormed over toward the spot on the lawn that had claimed her mother and Aunt Sandy.

Suddenly, she wondered if she was letting her emotions get the best of her.

She turned back to Avery. Before she could apologize, a tentacle yanked the axe out of her hand and flung it into Elijah's yard.

"Oh," said Chloe. Then she said it again. "Oh."

She didn't like that these tentacles kept learning new skills.

And now she was away from the "safety" of the tree and vulnerable.

Madison cried out.

The tentacles pulled her forward, and she fell off the tree. She screamed as they dragged her into the grass.

Avery rushed after her.

Before Avery could grab the other girl's feet, the tentacles pulled Madison underground.

They were getting much faster at this. *Practice makes perfect...?*

Chloe and Avery both screamed.

A bunch of tentacles, at least a dozen of them, burst up from the ground, surrounding Avery.

They pounced on her like hungry cobras.

She shouted and struggled, but Chloe could only watch helplessly as her best friend was pulled underground.

The lawn sealed up behind her as if it had never happened.

Chloe was the only one left.

The backyard was completely silent.

She had never felt more alone.

Perhaps this was her fate. She was destined to spend the rest of eternity walking around this backyard, all by herself. Punished for...what? Being a bad daughter? Being a bad friend?

She wanted to sit on the ground and weep.

What would happen if she went inside? Would she even know they needed help? She'd lost her note. She'd probably think they'd all abandoned her.

So many grim thoughts were floating around in her head that Chloe wished she could turn off her brain entirely.

She was snapped out of her dark thoughts when a tentacle grabbed her leg.

At least she wasn't destined to be alone for all eternity.

A million tentacles burst out of the ground. Okay, it wasn't a million, but it was a *lot*.

Chloe knew that it would do no good to scream and fight back. Still, that didn't stop her from screaming and fighting all the way down.

CHAPTER 16

Because she hadn't met the height requirement until recently, Chloe had only been on one roller coaster in her life. She'd screamed the entire way down the first hill, which made her stomach plunge, but it had been over quickly.

This was different. She fell and fell and fell...

...and fell...

...and fell...

As far as she could tell, the tentacles weren't pulling her anymore. She was plummeting by herself, surrounded by dirt, but the dirt wasn't putting up any resistance. It was definitely getting up her nose, though.

And then she landed.

She hit the bottom really hard, but it didn't shatter all her bones. She was only a bit shaken. She wiped the dirt out of her eyes and looked around.

It was dark but not pitch-black. She seemed to be in a very small cave. The lighting was odd, sort of a dark purple color.

A tentacle clamped down upon her shoulder, and she screamed.

"It's all right," said Aunt Sandy. "You're all right."

It wasn't a tentacle. It was Aunt Sandy's hand.

Aunt Sandy!

And Mom was right next to her!

So was Elijah. And Madison. And Avery, although she, like Chloe, seemed to still be processing what had happened to her.

Chloe gave Mom a hug and burst into tears. They held each other for a long moment. "Where are we?" Chloe finally asked.

"Shouldn't you say hi to me first?" said someone with a familiar deep voice.

Dad!

Chloe couldn't believe her eyes. It was really him! He needed a haircut, and he'd grown a thick beard, but it was him!

She was positively stunned. How could this be possible?

Granted, she lived in a world where tentacles could drag her belowground, so nothing should be *too* much of a surprise!

"You probably have a lot of questions," said Dad.

"You are very right about that." said Chloe, but she couldn't stop smiling. It was her dad. Alive!

"What we're going to do is have everybody take five minutes to hug and cry and get out all their emotions. Because after that, we're going to have to pull ourselves together and get a job done."

"What kind of a job?" asked Chloe.

"You're not going to like it."

"I assumed I wouldn't."

"Five minutes. Then I'll explain everything."

Chloe was pretty sure Dad ended up giving them ten. There were indeed hugs and relieved tears galore. She even hugged Elijah, who apologized for leaving them behind, even though it clearly was not his fault.

"All right, let's get started," said Dad. He looked at Chloe. "You know how I've always told you that I work in an office?"

"Yes."

"That's true. But you know how I've always told you that I work in marketing?"

"Yes..." Chloe exchanged glances with her friends.

"That's not true. I...study things. Things other people do not study. Things like, I don't know, ancient supernatural creatures that live beneath the surface of the earth."

Chloe gaped at him. "Did Mom know this?"

"Mom knew that I didn't work in marketing. She thought I was a spy."

"I would never have believed you were a spy," said Chloe.

"It doesn't matter, because I'm not. What does matter is that I got too close to discovering the truth about this creature, and it came after me. I don't know how long it was watching me, but it knew that I stopped at Virgil's Convenience Store on my way home from work every day for a candy bar."

"I didn't know you stopped for a candy bar every day," said Mom.

"It was my little secret."

"No, your *monster research* was your little secret," said Chloe.

"That was my big secret. I like candy bars, okay? I have since I was a kid. But if I brought one home for myself, I'd have to get one for both of you, and it would start to get expensive. I know it's not really healthy either, and I didn't want to have that discussion. I recognize that I'm getting off the subject, but I've been down here for a while and haven't had anyone to talk to until you all arrived."

"It's okay," said Chloe. "I'll buy you a candy bar as soon as we get out of here."

"My point is that Virgil's has a dirt parking lot, and I almost always get the space right in front of the store. I parked, and then these tentacles burst out of the dirt and started pulling the car into the ground. There was some guy standing ten feet away, looking right at me, but he didn't *see* me. He stood there making a phone call. And the next thing I knew, I was down here."

"With the car?"

"Yeah. No place to drive it, though. I knew you and your mother would be worried sick about me, and I hoped that somehow you'd find me, but when giant tentacles pull you and your car underground without a trace, it's kind of hard for the authorities to track you down."

"Didn't anybody you work with figure out what happened?" asked Elijah.

"Well, almost everybody I work with actually does do marketing work. The only other guy in monster research is Wally, and he hasn't shown up to rescue me." Dad frowned. "Am I bombarding you with a lot of information?"

"It's okay," said Chloe. "Tell us everything."

"From what I already knew about the creature, and from what I've learned by talking to each of you as you were pulled down here, the creature is in the process of increasing its power."

"Does the creature have a name?" asked Avery.

"Yes, but it's difficult to pronounce properly."

"Do you have a nickname for it?" asked Madison.

"Yes, but you won't be able to pronounce that either. I call it 'the creature' because I didn't ever discuss my work with anybody but Wally, so we never needed a cool name. We should come up with something."

"Fang Face?" suggested Elijah.

"We haven't seen fangs or its face," pointed out Avery.

"I vote we save the nickname for later," said Chloe.

"Anyway," Dad continued, "I think it's trying to increase its power, going after the people I love. Now that it has all of you, I think it's going to increase its hunting territory."

"To my yard?" asked Elijah, sounding really worried.

"Maybe. It's a slow process. It took a year after the creature brought me down here for it to come after you. But I think the process is going to get faster and faster, and its hunting territory is going to get larger and larger, until..."

"Until what?" asked Avery.

"I don't want to exaggerate. I'm not saying this thing can take over the whole world. I'm also, uh, not saying that it *can't* take over the whole world. I don't know where it plans to stop."

"So you're saying that our job is to save the world?" asked Chloe.

Dad nodded. "Sounds overly dramatic when you put it like that, but, yes, our job is to save the world."

"Wow," said Elijah.

"How do we beat this thing?" asked Chloe.

"Can I ask a question first?" asked Madison. "How have you been alive down here all this time?"

Dad turned and pointed. "Around that corner there's a pool of water. I'd offer you some, but it's very, very nasty. And I've been eating a lot of bugs. I mean, a *lot* of bugs. They're pretty big down here, so don't be startled if something scurries past your feet that's larger than the roaches you're used to."

"Have you really been eating bugs for months?" asked Mom.

Dad patted his belly. "Protein. I could really use some fruits and vegetables. And a candy bar."

"Back to saving the world," said Chloe.

"Yes, yes, back to that." Dad cleared his throat. "The creature can be hurt. We've heard you do it."

"It's way louder down here than it is up there," said Elijah.

"I'm told you've been fighting back fairly successfully."

"Obviously we haven't been fighting back *that* successfully because we're all down here now," said Chloe. "But, yeah, we chopped off a few tentacles."

"That's good," said Dad. "Although it has a few thousand tentacles. Maybe more."

"Where do you keep your axes?"

Dad smiled. "I wish it were that simple. While you were up there, how scared were you?"

"Super-duper scared."

"Of course you were. Why wouldn't you be? The thing is, the creature feeds on fear. That's the source of its power. You being scared is why those tentacles keep coming after you."

"If we'd stopped being scared, they would have left us alone?" asked Avery.

Dad nodded.

"Well, that would've been good to know sooner."

"I know," Dad admitted. "If I could've sent a message up there, I would have."

"I wasn't scared the whole time, though," said Chloe. "When we first decided that we were going to fight them, I was angry. I was furious. I've been angry since you left us, and I used that to help me fight."

"But were you scared at the same time?" Dad asked.

"Maybe? Probably."

"And were the others scared?"

Madison raised her hand. "I was definitely scared."

"To vanquish this monster—is the word 'vanquish' too melodramatic? I apologize if it is. But to vanquish it, we need to fight it in a completely fear-free environment. And that's going to be a challenge because the monster is really scary."

"Are you saying that not one of us is allowed to be scared?" asked Aunt Sandy.

"Yes."

"There are seven of us," said Avery. "All seven of us have to fight this creature that's going to take over the world... without being a teensy bit afraid?" She muttered something under her breath in Spanish that Chloe couldn't make out.

"A teensy bit might be okay," said Dad. "I haven't had the opportunity to test it. But if we march into battle with courage in our hearts, I believe we can win. If one or more of us get really scared, it will feed off that energy...and then it will feed on us."

"It'll eat us?" asked Madison.

"Right," said Dad. "But it has millions of teeth in its mouth, so you won't have time to suffer. It's not like you'll digest in its stomach or anything."

"Not doing a good job keeping us unafraid, Dad," said Chloe.

"I apologize."

"How do we stop ourselves from being scared?" asked Elijah. "Everybody knows I'm one of the bravest kids in the neighborhood, but when those tentacles came after me, I thought I was going to wet my pants. I almost did. So if I was scared then, and these teeth and tentacles sound much worse, how are we supposed to not be scared now?"

"That's a very good question," said Dad.

Everybody waited.

"Do you have a very good answer?" asked Chloe.

"Meditation."

"What?"

"We'll all get really relaxed. Close our eyes. Take deep breaths. Think happy thoughts. Become one with our surroundings, not that we have much in the way of surroundings to become one with. Tell everybody that we've got their backs. Get ourselves into a state where we're not afraid of anything. I'll lead some exercises, and when each person feels like they've completely let go of their fear, they'll raise their hand, and when all seven hands are in the air, we'll go fight it."

"That's what you came up with?" asked Chloe.

"Yes."

"After all these months?"

"I've been all alone down here! I didn't have anybody to brainstorm ideas with!"

"I don't think it's a terrible idea," said Mom. She gave his hand a squeeze in support.

"Sitting around doing breathing exercises isn't going to make me *not* scared," said Chloe.

"Well, they're visualization exercises too. There are a lot of different components to the process."

"That's really your best idea?"

Dad shrugged. "Do you have a better one?"

"Actually," said Chloe. "I think I do."

CHAPTER 17

Chloe, Avery, Madison, Elijah, Mom, Aunt Sandy, and Dad walked down the dark tunnel. They'd been walking through this tunnel for a very long time, and after her ordeal aboveground, Chloe was ready to take a break, but she didn't want to be the one to ask if they could stop.

"Can we stop for a minute?" asked Madison.

"Sure," said Dad. "Sorry, there's no comfortable place to sit. If you're hungry, there are plenty of bugs around. Just put your hand on the ground, and one will crawl into it. If you're not hungry, watch out. There are bugs all over the place."

Madison made a face.

"Where do these tunnels lead?" asked Avery.

"No place, really," said Dad. "They all dead-end, except

for the one we're following to the creature. There's one I made into my bedroom and one I made into my bathroom—you don't want to go in there—but for the most part, there's nothing to see."

"So what does the creature need with these tunnels?"

"I'm not completely sure. I think its plan is to keep collecting prisoners and draw from their fear, then eat them."

"I think it would be scarier if the light were red instead of purple," said Madison.

"I'll pass along the constructive criticism if I get the chance. Ready to walk again?"

They resumed the walk through the tunnel, little groups having their own quiet conversations.

"What did I miss while I was down here?" Dad asked Chloe.

"Some stuff."

"I'm so sorry, honey."

"It wasn't your fault."

"I know, but I'll make it up to you. I promise."

"I'll tell you what: if we save the world, we'll call it even."

"Deal. Also, I'll buy you some ice cream."

A six-inch centipede scurried over Chloe's bare foot,

but she didn't even care. They were on a mission. And her mom and dad were here, and they were together and safe...for now.

A few minutes later, she asked, "Is that the car?"

She didn't really need to ask. Of course it was their car. Her intention was simply to point out that Dad's car was in the middle of this underground tunnel.

"Yep," said Dad. "I think the creature brought it to make the mystery of my disappearance more beguiling."

"Does the creature think that way?" asked Mom. "Clever."

"I don't know. Maybe. It's an ancient evil that doesn't talk, so it's hard to say."

"We should use it," said Chloe.

"There's no way to drive it to get out," said Dad. "All these tunnels are dead ends."

"We could drive it to the creature!"

"There's not much farther to walk. No need to be lazy."

"What I'm saying is we could drive it *into* the creature!"

Dad thought about that for a moment. "That's...not an idea I'd considered. It has merit."

"I call the front seat," said Elijah.

"Oh, I wanted to sit next to you," Madison mumbled.

"Let's not get too hasty. The car might not even start."

Still, they all climbed in. Dad had conveniently left the keys in the vehicle. He turned the ignition. After a few tries, it started.

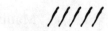

The car was intended to seat four people comfortably and five people uncomfortably. Dad and Mom rode up front, while Aunt Sandy, Madison, and Elijah squeezed into the back seat. Chloe and Avery walked behind them. It was easy to keep up, because Dad drove very slowly.

"I'm so glad your dad's okay. Somehow I always thought he would be," Avery said to Chloe.

It was true. Avery had never once said, *It's time to accept reality.* She'd always tried to help Chloe cling to hope. This had made Chloe angry at a certain point, as if her friend were trying to prevent her from moving forward with her life, but she was glad she'd never let it come between them.

Chloe smiled. "Yeah, it's pretty cool. I wish he'd just come in through the front door, though."

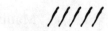

Dad stopped the car and turned off the headlights. Everybody got out.

"Okay," said Dad. "The creature is beyond the darkness ahead."

"That sounds scary," said Elijah.

"Stop thinking like that. We can't let it feed on our fear. This is an adventure! So much fun!"

"It sounds mega-fun," said Elijah.

"I couldn't beat it alone, but I believe that the seven of us, working together, can do it."

"You only believe we can?" asked Mom. "You're not positive?"

Aunt Sandy looked skeptical too, and she pulled Madison into a hug.

"It's a gigantic beast! But we can do it."

"What percentage chance do you think we have?" asked Aunt Sandy, who'd been quieter than usual.

"That's not important," said Dad. "This isn't about whether we have a three percent chance or a four percent chance. We have a chance! It's not impossible! We can save the world!"

"I really don't like that your highest chance of survival was four percent," said Chloe.

"There's really no reason to talk numbers because they're irrelevant. The important thing is that I believe in us. I really, truly do."

"Then let's do this," said Avery.

"I'm going to get us all into a state of calm. And then we'll get back in the car and—"

"I want to drive," said Chloe.

"Excuse me?"

"I want to drive. It was my idea to use the car, and I want to drive."

"You don't have your driver's license," said Dad.

"Do you think I'm gonna get pulled over down here?"

"Since when do you know how to drive?"

"I know how to drive in a straight line. That's all we're doing, right? Driving in a straight line?"

Dad nodded. "That is indeed all we're doing. Okay then. Everybody stand in a circle and hold hands. Let's get started."

/////

Fine. Chloe would give Dad some credit. His meditation was making her feel less frightened.

He spoke in a very soft, soothing voice, the kind he'd used when she'd been much younger. He'd sit on the edge of her bed and assure her that there were no monsters under there. (Apparently, they were under the yard instead.)

It seemed to be working on the others too, though it wasn't as if she knew what was going on in their minds. But nobody was a whimpering, blubbering mess.

Dad talked for so long that she started to get bored. Maybe that was part of his plan: make them so bored that they couldn't be scared. Her mind wandered.

It was hard to keep track of time down here, so she wasn't sure how long it had been—approximately forever—before Dad said, "I think we're ready. Chloe, do you feel calm and unafraid?"

"Yes."

"Madison, do you feel calm and unafraid?"

"Yes."

One by one, everybody answered yes. Chloe hoped nobody was fibbing.

"Good," said Dad. "Then let us peacefully and bravely proceed."

Chloe didn't think this plan was especially peaceful.

The concept was straightforward: if they went into its

lair without fear, it wouldn't be able to fight back. So, even though the only weapons they had were what Dad had scavenged out of the car (a tire iron, four hubcaps, a screwdriver, and a few other things), they should be able to destroy it.

Oh, but they'd have to do it with their eyes closed. Because apparently if they *looked* at this thing, there was no possibility of not being scared.

Chloe got into the driver's seat. Dad had let her drive before. Not out on the open road, but in an empty parking lot. Once. It had been awesome. And now all she had to do was hold the wheel straight and press the gas pedal to the floor. She could handle that. She was pretty sure she could handle that.

Earlier, they'd rolled down all the windows and then smashed out the front and rear windshields so no glass would spray at them upon impact. That part had been kind of fun. They'd used the tire iron.

Avery sat next to her. The adults had wanted to do this part, but for Chloe's idea to work, she'd insisted that she needed to be with her friends.

Elijah and Madison were in the back seat. Mom, Aunt Sandy, and Dad would follow behind on foot.

Everybody put on their seat belts.

"Are we ready to party?" Chloe asked.

"Yeah!" said Avery.

"Then close your eyes and picture this thing in its underwear!"

While Dad's soothing meditation had helped dispel some of the fear, there was no way to know if that would last. Chloe's belief was that they needed to turn this all into one big joke. Make one another laugh. Do all the silly stuff that would get them in trouble at school. It was hard to be scared when you were being funny and goofing off.

The adults would put on their own comedy routine behind them. But Chloe thought they'd have the greatest chance of success if there were just kids in the car. They could be funniest together.

"Who has the worst breath?" asked Avery. "Maybe that's how we'll beat it."

"Me!" said Elijah. "I have the worst breath! Wanna smell?"

"Want to see my impression of the monster?" asked Madison. She put her finger against her nose, pretending to pick it. "Hur hur hur! I'm the monster! Hur hur hur!"

"That's the most accurate impression I've ever seen," said Chloe. She pretended to pick her own nose. "Durrrr! Look at me! I can pick my nose with a thousand different arms!"

"Maybe it's a great big clown nose," said Madison.

"What if it honks when we slam the car into it?" asked Chloe.

"No, not a nose," said Avery. "Maybe it's a snorty pug with tentacles. And we're not supposed to look at it because it's so cute that we'll want to pet it."

"I hope it's not a clown pug," said Madison.

"I bet it says 'aw, man!' a lot," said Elijah. "So, when we hit it with the car, it's going to be all like, 'Aw, man!' but with a really high-pitched voice, like, *'Aw, man! Why'd you go and do that? Why'd you bonk your car into me? I was just tryin' to pick my nose. You didn't even bring me a tissue. Aw, man!'*"

Everybody laughed. This was not brilliant comedic material, but it was getting the job done.

They were ready.

Chloe slammed her foot on the gas pedal, then squeezed her eyes shut.

CHAPTER 18

The car shot forward.

Chloe braced herself.

According to Dad, the creature was just beyond the darkness, so the car should hit it any second now.

She wasn't scared.

She couldn't believe she wasn't scared.

Time to save the world!

There was a huge jolt as the car struck something. Chloe jerked forward, but she was wearing her seat belt and didn't fly through the windshield.

Much to her surprise, the car kept moving. A lot slower, but still moving.

Why was the car still moving?

And what was pouring onto her?

"Did we just...?" asked Avery.

Yes. They certainly had. When they hit the creature, the car didn't crash as they'd anticipated. It had gone *right into it*. They were driving around *inside* the creature.

The stuff pouring down on them was probably black ooze, although it felt more like sludge.

"Everybody hold your breath!" she shouted.

Chloe kept the accelerator pressed to the floor and turned the steering wheel to the right. She wasn't sure how long the car could drive inside an ancient beast, but she wanted to do as much damage as possible.

She turned to the left.

Back to the right.

Did this thing have any bones? It didn't seem like it.

She couldn't breathe. It was like driving underwater.

What if they got trapped inside the creature? Would their parents be able to rescue them?

She *immediately* put that thought out of her mind. No scary thoughts allowed. This was fun. This was better than the best theme park ride! They could get rich charging admission for this!

Suddenly the car swerved in the opposite direction than she'd been steering. As far as Chloe could tell, the creature was moving around. It was probably unhappy that there was a car driving inside it.

Chloe turned to the left.

Then to the right again.

What would it feel like to have a car driving through your guts? Probably not very good.

She felt a gentle touch on her arm. Just Avery, trying to be reassuring. She couldn't actually *say* anything reassuring because they were drowning in sludge.

No, not drowning. Partying! They were partying in sludge!

Chloe tried to think of every knock-knock joke she'd ever heard. It was starting to become difficult to hold her breath.

Chloe hoped Madison and Elijah were okay. She really hoped they hadn't swallowed any of the creature's insides. That would probably be deadly poison, and also disgusting.

The front of the car began to rise. It got higher and higher until Chloe worried that they were all going to spill out of it. She wasn't sure they'd be able to swim out of the creature. She wanted to put the car into reverse but couldn't find the gearshift in all the muck.

If they didn't get out of here soon, like in the next few seconds, she was going to suffocate.

She'd lost her sense of direction and had no idea how to best get out of here, so all she could do was floor the accelerator and hope for the best.

There was a jolt as the car hit something. The creature let out a shriek that Chloe thought would've made her eardrums explode if they weren't completely immersed in the slime. Maybe the car had run into something important...?

The car continued to move forward. Then they jolted forward again as the car hit something else. Whatever they struck this time didn't give way like the creature's skin.

Now the car was completely stopped.

But she could hear the sludge pouring *out* of the open windows. She opened the door to make the process go faster. She could breathe again!

It sounded like Avery, Madison, and Elijah also opened their doors.

Chloe wiped some gunk out of her eyes.

The creature's shriek was fading, like it was dying. Had they hit its brain? Its heart? Its lungs? Some otherworldly body part that humans didn't even have? Or was it simply that having a full-size automobile driving around inside its guts had eventually destroyed it?

It didn't matter. Chloe breathed a sigh of relief.

Then she screamed. The car flew upward, as if it had been resting on a giant spring.

The other kids screamed as well.

When Chloe opened her eyes again, she was looking at the top of her house. As in, she was looking straight ahead at the top of her house. As in, she was in the air, as high as her house.

The car seemed to hover in midair for a moment, and then it fell, making her stomach feel like it dropped at a different speed than her body.

It crashed onto the lawn.

For a moment Chloe just sat there, trying to figure out what had happened.

"Are you okay?" asked Avery.

"I—I might be."

Avery looked into the back seat. "Madison? Elijah?"

"We're not dead," said Elijah.

"Chloe!" shouted Mom.

Mom, Dad, and Aunt Sandy climbed out of a very large hole in the backyard and hurried over to the vehicle. They helped the kids out. Everybody was completely drenched in the black goo, so it was impossible to gauge the extent of their injuries, but nobody was rolling around on the ground while screaming in agony. They'd all be okay. The sun was shining, they were home, and they'd all be okay.

There was a lot of hugging, despite the slime.

"What happened?" asked Chloe.

"I think we beat it," said Dad.

"We killed it?"

Dad frowned. At least it looked like he frowned—it was hard to tell with all the ooze. "I don't know for sure. But it clearly didn't want us down there anymore. I'm going to take that as a win. For now, we saved the world." He smiled for certain. "By which I mean *you* saved the world. Thanks, Chloe. Thanks, kids."

"Happy to help, Mr. Whitting," said Avery.

"Wow," said Dad. "The whole tree came down, huh?"

"Yep," said Chloe.

"Sorry about your tree house. Maybe it's time for you to have your own car." He patted the steaming crumpled hood of the automobile, which looked like it would never drive again. "Enjoy your new ride."

"Thanks, Dad."

Everybody did some more hugging. Madison gave Elijah a big hug, which made him grin.

Then came a shout from next door. "Elijah?" Mrs. Duncan

called, "I've been looking all over for you!" She hurried into their backyard. "What...what exactly...what...?"

"There's a lot to explain, Mom."

Elijah's mother could see what was really happening in their backyard! The creature's illusion was gone. Things were back to normal.

Maybe the police would be here soon—unless they'd already shown up and left. It didn't matter. Dad was back. The landscaping bill wasn't Chloe's concern. She'd probably get nervous whenever she saw an octopus from now on, but she didn't see octopi very often, so that was no big deal.

"Your backyard campout was awful," said Avery. "But thanks for inviting me."

"Thanks for inviting me too," said Madison. "I know I wasn't really invited, but thanks for letting me join you."

"I wasn't invited either," said Elijah, "but I enjoyed fighting tentacles with you. It sure wasn't boring."

"You're all invited to the next campout," Chloe told them.

"Hear me out," said Avery, "instead of camping out in a tent in your backyard, maybe we stay inside and watch movies."

"That's a great idea," said Chloe. Then, with a laugh, she added, "Now, who wants to go for a drive in my new car?"

ACKNOWLEDGMENTS

Thanks to Tod Clark, Donna Fitzpatrick, Marcia Gonzales, Jamie LaChance, Michael McBride, Jim Morey, Bridgett Nelson, Annette Pollert-Morgan, and Paul Synuria II for their spoooooooky assistance with this book!

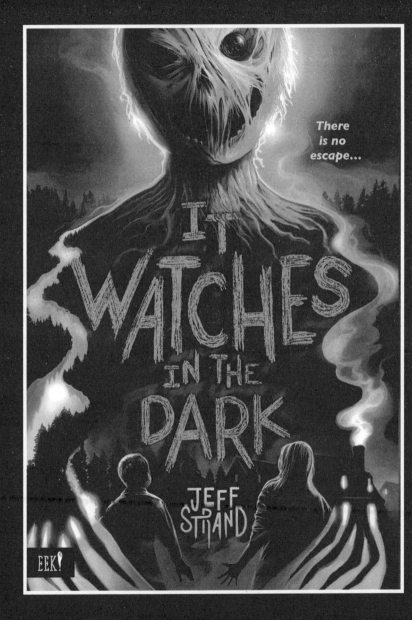

Photo © Lynne Hansen

ABOUT THE AUTHOR

Jeff Strand is a Bram Stoker Award-winning author with more than fifty books to his credit. *Cemetery Dance* magazine said, "no author working today comes close to Jeff Strand's perfect mixture of comedy and terror." Several of his books are in development as movies. He lives in Minnesota. Visit his gleefully macabre website at www.JeffStrand.com.

IT WATCHES IN THE DARK

CHAPTER ONE

"Hold on," said Dad. "It's gonna get a bit rough."

Oliver adjusted his life vest, even though it was perfectly snug already. He held on to his seat in the middle of the canoe with both hands. He wasn't scared—not yet—but those rapids up ahead looked worse than anything they'd anticipated on this trip.

"Do you want to trade places?" he asked Trisha, who sat in front of him. He hoped she'd say no.

His twin sister glanced back at him and smiled. "Nope, I'm fine."

Oliver breathed a sigh of relief.

Dad sat in the back, so he was responsible for steering. For most of the trip, he'd relaxed in the center seat, letting

Oliver and Trisha paddle and steer. They were good at it—they spent every other weekend with Dad, and these weekends almost always involved some time on the water.

"Everybody down," said Dad.

Oliver and Trisha knelt on the bottom of the canoe. This was to lower their center of gravity and make it less likely that the canoe would tip over in the rough water. Dad didn't sound worried, so Oliver decided he wouldn't worry either. Everything would be fine. The violently churning water up ahead was no big deal.

"It'll be okay," Dad assured them. "Worst-case scenario, our stuff gets wet."

Of course, there were many scenarios worse than water getting into the canoe. They could lose their gear. Or get dragged along the rocky river bottom by the current. Or eaten by a great white shark that had gotten lost. Or, you know, *drown*. Even if you stuck to the plausible scenarios, there were many, many, many things worse than spending the night in a damp sleeping bag.

Oliver hoped Trisha was too busy paddling to glance back at him because he was sure he looked frightened. Not that she'd make fun of him, but still...

Trisha glanced back. "Don't be scared."

"I'm not," he insisted.

"We'll be fine."

"I know."

And they would be. Dad wouldn't have taken them on this adventure if they weren't ready. Mom would never have allowed it. It was slightly rougher water than they'd anticipated, sure, but they'd be through it quickly, and the knot in Oliver's stomach would disappear. Then they could eat lunch.

Even if Dad wasn't there, Oliver and Trisha would've been fine. They worked well together in a canoe. Most people would say, "Well, of course! They're twins!" But Oliver and Trisha got on each other's nerves more often than they finished each other's sentences. They didn't share a secret language or feel pain when the other one stubbed their toe, or anything like that. Being in sync while paddling the canoe came from hours and hours of practice, not any kind of psychic twin bond.

They didn't have many common interests either. Oliver was into books and video games, while Trisha was into sports and more sports. Still, they both loved being out on the water with their father.

Dad hadn't stopped grinning since he'd picked them up. Actually, he hadn't stopped grinning since Mom had (reluctantly) given him permission to take them on a five-day trip down the Champion River for their twelfth birthday. And the trip, now in the early afternoon of its third day, was going great. Sleeping in a tent every night! Campfires! Ghost stories! S'mores!

When they got home, they'd have the usual "birthday cake and presents" party with their friends, but it wouldn't be nearly as much fun.

"Listen for my instructions," said Dad, raising his voice over the rushing water.

And then they were in the rapids.

It was like being on a wet roller coaster. Water sprayed Oliver's face, getting in his eyes. At least it wasn't salt water. He blinked the water out.

"Paddle hard!" Dad shouted over the roar of the river.

Oliver held his breath, his grip tightening on the seat. A quick turn, and they narrowly missed a tree branch that jutted into the river.

Another quick maneuver, and they navigated between some large rocks, picking up speed as they went.

Everyone in the boat was focused. They were almost through the worst of it. It was going to be totally fine. A few more yards and—

The canoe jolted as if the Loch Ness Monster had risen beneath it. But it wasn't Nessie—they'd struck a huge rock.

The canoe spun.

Then it flipped.

Oliver had been splashed by the water constantly during this trip and even sometimes trailed his hand in the river, but he wasn't prepared for just how *cold* it felt to plunge into it.

In some places, the Champion River was over his head, and in some places, it wasn't. He gripped his life jacket and frantically kicked his feet, hoping to touch the bottom. He couldn't. He was carried off with the current, followed by the overturned canoe.

He looked around, trying not to panic. They'd practiced what to do if they capsized, but he couldn't see Trisha or Dad.

"Oliver!" Trisha screamed.

He still couldn't see her, but her voice came from the other side of the canoe. He grabbed for it and missed.

Oliver spat out some water. "I'm okay!"

Where was Dad?

Oliver tried to grab the canoe and missed again. It slid ahead of him, and he saw Trisha desperately holding on to the other side.

There was no sign of Dad. They were all wearing bright orange life jackets, but Oliver couldn't see one bobbing in the water around him. Was Dad submerged? Behind them? Dad could be anywhere.

How long had it been? Twenty seconds? Dad could hold his breath for twenty seconds, no problem.

Oliver's shoes scraped along the river bottom. He tried to stop his forward momentum, but the water was still too fast and too deep.

Trisha and the canoe were getting farther and farther away.

Oliver tried to scream for their father but got a mouthful of cold water. He coughed and sputtered, then scanned the river again.

There! He caught a glimpse of orange in the water!

It was about ten feet behind him. Though Oliver was floating down the middle of the river, Dad (that *had* to be Dad!) was much closer to the edge.

Oliver couldn't see the orange anymore.

No! There it was! Dad bobbed to the surface. But it wasn't Dad smiling and waving at him. He was facedown, letting the river's current carry him along.

Oliver swam toward him. He wasn't super athletic, and

swimming across the current would be a challenge for any-body, but he had to do this!

He felt like his arms were on fire, even in the freezing water, but he pushed harder.

He was getting closer. Closer.

Closer...

He grabbed Dad by the vest. Oliver tried to turn him over, to get his face out of the water, but it was difficult enough to hold on to him.

"Oliver!"

He looked over at Trisha. She'd righted the canoe, run it up the riverbank, and was holding out her paddle. If he missed it, he and Dad would be swept along the river for who knew how long.

Trisha waded into the river, extending the paddle.

Clinging to Dad's vest, Oliver reached for it.

Got it!

He pulled Dad onto his back, but his life jacket was slip-ping out of Oliver's grasp. He couldn't lose him now!

The paddle slid out of Oliver's numb fingers, and the two were swept forward. Oliver tried to dig his feet into the dirt and rocks of the riverbed to slow them down. It wasn't working.

Oliver didn't give up. He could do this. He knew he could do this. He was *not* going to let go of Dad. They were *not* going to be carried down the river to their doom.

And then, not too far past Trisha, it started to work. The water was smoother and not as deep. They both slowed, giving Oliver a chance to breathe.

He wanted to say something reassuring, but his teeth were chattering too much for him to speak. He dragged Dad to the edge of the river, where Trisha hurried over to meet them. Together they pulled their father out of the water.

Dad slumped over to the side. His eyes were closed. Water spilled down his face, and then it turned red.

"Is he okay?" Oliver asked, barely able to get out the words. "Is he breathing?"

"I—I think so? I can't tell!" Trisha pressed her fingers into Dad's wrist. "I think he has a pulse."

"You *think*?"

"He's freezing, and my hands are freezing!" She waited a moment. "Okay, there's definitely a pulse. And he's breathing."

Oliver was so relieved that he wanted to burst into tears.

"Go get the first aid kit from the canoe," said Trisha.

Normally, Oliver didn't like being ordered around by his sister, but she was absolutely right. He ran over to the canoe.

The first aid kit had been strapped down, so he unfastened and grabbed it, then ran back to Trisha and Dad.

"Thanks," said Trisha, opening it.

As she took out some gauze, Oliver pulled his cell phone out of his pocket and removed it from the protective bag. They were deep in the wilderness, and it was possible there was no signal out here, but he'd hope for the best.

He turned on the phone and waited a few excruciating moments for it to power up. When it did, he had no bars.

"I'm going to see if I can find a signal," he told Trisha. She nodded, focused on their father.

Shivering, Oliver walked along the riverbank, holding the phone up in the air as if getting it three feet higher might make the difference. Both sides of the river were thick forest—clearly nobody lived around here. Wandering through the woods in the hope of stumbling upon help would be a useless effort.

He kept walking while Trisha patched up Dad's head wound, but he hurried back when she called out that she was finished.

"Anything?" she asked.

Oliver shook his head. "How bad was it?"

"It wasn't *good*," said Trisha. "But I think he'll be okay. We need to get him to a doctor as soon as possible."

"Let's get him in the canoe and keep going down the river. If we don't find a phone signal, we'll at least see a house or cabin." It had been a while since they'd passed one, but it wasn't as if they were deep in a remote area of the Amazon. They were in Missouri. If they kept floating down the river, they'd come across someone before too long.

Fortunately, it wasn't that difficult to maneuver Dad into the canoe, even while needing to be extremely careful. Oliver was nobody's idea of a super athlete, but he could help lift Dad without accidentally dropping him.

Trisha, meanwhile, *was* a super athlete. Also, she'd begun her growth spurt. Oliver wasn't a big fan of being three inches shorter than his twin sister, but he'd catch up eventually.

"It's going to be fine, Dad," said Trisha. "We'll find help, I promise."

Dad did not respond.

They resumed the trip, though it was no longer any fun. Oliver's heart was racing as much as it had in the rapids.

"He'll be fine," Trisha told Oliver. "I bet he'll wake up soon."

"His head was bleeding pretty bad. And what if he gets hypothermia?"

"It looked worse than it really was. We'll probably have to stop him from grabbing a paddle. He'll want to make up for the time we lost."

Oliver didn't like that his sister—who was technically thirteen minutes younger—was trying to hide the reality of their situation from him as if he were a little kid. Or maybe she was trying to hide it from herself.

As they paddled down the river, Oliver kept an eye on his cell phone, waiting for a mere one bar to show up on the display. Enough for emergency services to track their location and send a helicopter. Not that there was anywhere to land a helicopter—they'd probably have to lower a stretcher on a rope to whisk him away.

What if they didn't find anybody before nightfall? What if Dad stayed unconscious? It would be too dangerous to canoe down the river after dark. He needed medical attention now.

Dad let out a soft moan but didn't open his eyes.

Trisha's back was to Oliver, but he heard her sniffle. Oliver couldn't think of anything reassuring to say.

They didn't speak for a while. Oliver was suddenly struck by the fear that there might be even worse rapids ahead, rapids that would catapult Dad right out of the canoe.

Stop that, he told himself. *Focus on the immediate problem.*

They continued down the river. Adrenaline coursed through Oliver's body, but his arms were getting tired. Where were the people? Where were the other boats? Oliver wanted to scream at his phone to find a signal, but that wouldn't do any good, and he didn't want Trisha to think he couldn't handle a crisis. If she could stay calm, so could he.

He kept checking on Dad, making sure he was still breathing. Why wouldn't he wake up? If he had an internet connection, Oliver could google how long it took somebody to regain consciousness after they'd been knocked out.

"There!" Trisha shouted as Oliver saw it himself. A large wooden dock! Though it wasn't in the best shape, it didn't look completely abandoned. There was a rowboat tied there. A rowboat wasn't nearly as useful as a speedboat, but it showed that somebody was actually using the dock.

A trail led into the trees. Maybe there was a cabin out of view.

A cabin didn't mean there'd be anybody inside to help, but at least this was *something*.

They paddled the canoe until it gently bumped against the dock. Trisha got out.

"You stay with Dad," she said. "I'll see if I can find somebody."

"No. We'll both go."

"We can't leave him alone."

"Why not?" Oliver asked. "Nobody's going to kidnap him. I'm not going to let you walk through the woods alone."

He didn't like seeing all the cobwebs in the rowboat. It was a pretty clear sign nobody had used it recently, but he wasn't going to point that out.

Trisha was also looking into the rowboat, and he wondered if she'd come to the same conclusion. "What if somebody comes down the river while we're gone and we miss them?"

"Dad's unconscious in a canoe with his head all bandaged. They'll stop to see what's wrong. You're not going by yourself. I'm not debating it."

"All right," said Trisha. "But let's hurry."

Oliver got out of the canoe, and they slid it up on shore, then firmly tied it to the dock. Dad wasn't going anywhere.

"Everything's going to be all right," he said to Dad before hurrying up the trail with Trisha. Oliver only wished he believed it.